Halloween Hayride Murder

Linnea West

●Chapter 1●

The red and orange leaves were swirling down Main Street, pushed by a chilly October wind that made me shiver even though I was sitting safe and warm in The Donut Hut. I was eating an orange donut with sprinkles shaped like little bats. I tried my hardest not to satisfy my eternal sweet tooth, but I am a sucker for anything seasonal and Mandy knows that. Mandy is my best friend, who runs The Donut Hut and, like me, loves anything seasonal.

That is why we were both eating donuts right now actually. Mandy had offered up her space for a meeting of the Halloween Hayride Committee. Every October, our small town Shady Lake hosts a hayride to fill our coffers for the upcoming holiday season and all of the other holidays that don't make money on their own, like the Fourth of July fireworks.

Shady Lake is not just any small town. It's a small town that loves to throw a party. Every month, every season, every holiday has some sort of celebration here. People often wonder why in the world people live in Minnesota, but I can tell you why.

Minnesota has four distinct seasons and we know how to enjoy each of them.

Growing up in Shady Lake was absolutely magical. Winter has a large Christmas celebration when we light the Christmas tree downtown and a large Snow-lebration where we celebrate everything snow. Spring brings a big Easter egg roll in Central Park and the planting of the community garden. Summer has all sorts of outdoor activities because most of the parks are open for kids once school is out. They have penny carnivals and bike parades to keep the kids busy.

But my favorite season is autumn. The leaves slowly change colors, giving a final burst of happiness before winter starts. After sweating all summer, the temperatures finally drop and I can wear my favorite sweaters and scarves. And I love Halloween. I have since I was little.

The Halloween Hayride is a popular event because we make sure it is fun for all ages. It is a little bit scary to keep the older children interested, but not enough to scare the younger ones too much. Shady Lake had been hosting this event for decades and it actually pulls in people from all over the area, not just townies. It seems to get bigger

every year.

To prepare for the committee meeting, we had pushed all of the tables in the middle of the diner together so we could all sit together. Before everyone arrived, I was helping Mandy put trays of Halloween donuts and carafes of diner coffee on the table. The Hayride committee actually met monthly year-round to touch base on ideas, but now that it was October, we would be meeting twice weekly as we ramped up for the actual event.

Ding Ding

The bell over the door rang as it was pushed open. A short, balding man in a sweater vest came through the door followed by a tall woman in a drab brown sweatsuit. Ronald Green was the mayor of Shady Lake and unlike some small town mayors, he actually got involved in things because he loved them instead of just because he wanted the publicity. He sat on or led the committees for every activity Shady Lake throws. Sometimes I wonder when he has time to get anything else done.

His wife, on the other hand, was the opposite. Melinda had always been a sourpuss who seemed to hate Shady Lake despite living here her entire life. Actually,

Melinda seemed to hate everything. Obviously I had been pretty young when they got married, but no one quite understood what they saw in each other. It was the oddest pairing, yet they managed to stay together. Where Ronald was jolly and in the public eye, Melinda was drab and stayed in the shadows.

"I'm just not sure why the meeting has to take place in a donut shop," Melinda was saying with contempt as they walked in. "You certainly don't need any donuts. Remember, you are supposed to be losing that gut. Not adding more donut rolls to it."

I looked over at Mandy, who I could tell was thinking the exact same thing I was. We exchanged a look that was supposed to convey an eye roll without actually rolling our eyes. Poor Ronald.

"Oh Melly," Ronald said with a laugh. "You know that I am trying to lose weight. I just can't keep my hands off of those sweets sometimes. But I promise tonight I won't have one."

Ronald looked up and seemed to realize for the first time that Mandy and I were in the room. He smiled a broad smile and waved one large, meaty hand at us. Melinda was always nagging him about his weight, but I don't think Ronald could really be Ronald if he lost too much weight. He had always been a big teddy bear of a man.

"Hello ladies," he said excitedly. Melinda shot us one last look before exiting the donut shop. "I am so excited to really get the Hayride plans together. Thank you for hosting, Mandy. I'm sorry that I won't be able to partake in your delicious donuts tonight."

"Oh that's quite alright," Mandy said. She was the perfect picture of politeness. Thankfully I kept my mouth shut this time, unlike usual when I would say what I was thinking which was that maybe Melinda needed to have a few donuts to try and add some sweetness to her personality.

Ronald busied himself with setting up papers and a little whiteboard on a stand while Mandy and I finished up getting napkins, creamers, and sugar. The bell rang once again and I turned, wondering who the other early bird was showing up to the meeting.

Strolling through the door with a folder under his arm was Clark Hutchins. Clark is a high school social studies teacher who is probably one of the most handsome men

I've ever seen in real life. He didn't grow up in Shady Lake, which means he is a hot commodity. But somehow I've managed to have a few dates with him and while I'm not ready for monogamous dating yet, Clark is at the top of my list when I am ready. For now, we are just keeping it casual.

A beautiful stranger moving to town and actually taking an interest in me is the total opposite of anything that would have happened in high school. In high school, Mandy and I mostly hung out together and had a lot of crushes and a few awkward first dates. I had dated Max Marcus but then I had gone away to college where I ended up meeting my first husband Peter. Mandy had stayed behind and started dating Trevor, a boy we had gone to school with.

"Hey Tessa," Clark said as his eyes twinkled at me. I kind of wanted to melt a little bit inside. The only other time I had felt like this was when I first met Peter. It was the same feeling of someone I hadn't known my entire life actually taking an interest in me. The problem with dating in Shady Lake is that often you already know everything about each other. It isn't as fun to go out if there is nothing to talk about.

"Hi Clark. I see you've come prepared," I said, motioning to the folder in his hand.

"Yes I did," he said with a cute little chuckle. "You'll just have to wait until the meeting to see my evil plan."

As Clark walked by me, he reached out grabbed my hand to give it a quick squeeze. I smiled a big idiotic grin at him and was rewarded with one of his dazzling smiles. I felt my face starting to get warm as he found a spot to sit at the table.

The bell over the door continued to chime as the other members of the Hayride committee came in and found their spots. The room slowly filled up with chatter and laughter. Every time the door opened, a small draft of cool breeze came in with it. With every shiver from the cold air, I was inwardly delighted. I love fall and I'm pretty sure nothing can spoil this season for me.

•Chapter 2•

"Alright everyone, I know we're all busy stuffing our face with these delicious donuts, but we should really get down to business," said Ronald. While he was right about most of us, I know for a fact he was not stuffing his face with donuts. His love for Melinda must be pretty strong to avoid Mandy's donuts.

"We've done a pretty good job this year of preparing ahead of time, but today is the first of October which means we really need to nail down the details of this year's Halloween Hayride," Ronald said after the chatter died down.

When I moved back to town a few months ago, Mandy had roped me into helping out. She knew I loved Halloween and that I needed something to take my mind off of the car accident that had killed my husband over a year ago and forced me to move back to town. I had to admit, this was a pretty good distraction. It was always a challenge to take something that was a town staple and felt like it shouldn't be meddled with, but find a way to keep it fresh.

This year, we came up with the perfect idea to keep it fresh: a haunted house put on by the high school student council. It would be quite a bit scarier than the hayride, which was for all ages. The haunted house was going to be homespun, but also gory and scary.

I shouldn't say we came up with the idea. I hadn't had anything to do with it. Clark came up with it and we all agreed that it was a fantastic idea. That might have been because Clark was such a fantastic guy. Not only was he a devoted social studies teacher, he was also a high school football coach and the faculty supervisor for the student council. He loved what he did and it showed.

I glanced at Clark, who was sitting across the table from me. Ronald was giving a rundown on everything we had already done and what we still had to do for a few of the members who never bothered to show up to the meetings until October started. Clark had a very serious look on his face as he listened, but when he caught me looking at me, he gave me a smirk and a little wink that threw me off balance.

"Okay, Tessa, could you do your bit now?" Ronald said suddenly. I could feel that my cheeks were red and for a moment, I had no idea what he was talking about. Then I realized he wanted me to give my report. I was the publicity chair for the event.

"Oh yeah, sure," I said as I pushed my chair back and stood up. "Hello everyone. Well here we are in October with the Hayride just around the corner. This is when my job really starts."

Further down the table, I could see Chelsea Goodman rolling her eyes. She hadn't liked me since middle school when we had some squabble that I had since forgotten, but she had held on to it and seethed about it to this day. Her naturally red hair matched the fire that seemed to spout from her ears when I was around. Chelsea was here as a reporter for the town's newspaper, but also because she had the hots for Clark. I couldn't blame her though. I mean, who didn't have the hots for Clark?

"No worries, I have a sheet here with my marketing plan and I've made enough copies for everyone," I said as I slid the sheets around the table. I had worked in marketing when I lived in the Cities before Peter had died and, while I was perfectly happy working the front desk of my family's B&B, it was nice to use my marketing skills for good.

I walked the group step by step through the plan for sending flyers home with the elementary kids and a newspaper campaign, which Chelsea rolled her eyes at. I was actually quite proud of some of the innovative ideas I had included and just as I was getting to the best part, the door of The Donut Hut slammed open and a greasy looking little man who I had never seen before walked in followed by a hulking figure. The difference in their size was comical and made them look more like a cartoon duo than real life people.

I looked around the table and realized I was the only person who didn't seem to recognize them. Chelsea's eyes were the size of dinner plates and Clark's face had turned to stone. Even the always affable Ronald wasn't smiling anymore.

"Oh hello," the little man said. "I was pretty sure I had said I would need to be invited to the meetings, didn't I, Ralph?"

The large figure, who was apparently named Ralph, made an affirmative sort of grunt as he pulled a chair up to the table for the small man.

"Well here I am," he continued as he sat down and crossed his legs. "So if you are finished with your portion, sweetie, I would like to have a chance to talk."

"Who are you?" I blurted out. I had a bad habit of blurting out things I should have kept inside. Mandy gave an almost imperceptible shake of her head. She was always telling me that if I just kept my mouth shut for an extra ten seconds, that it would save me from embarrassment most of the time. Obviously, I still haven't taken her advice. The little man stared at me hard with his beady eyes, seemingly incensed that I didn't know who he was.

I stood there like an idiot while I tried to figure out what had just happened and what I was supposed to do about it. Clark rose to his feet, trying to stay cool and collected. I could tell the fury was barely being masked by the way he was twitching his fingers almost into fists, but not quite. He did the same thing whenever the football team made a stupid mistake.

"Excuse me Earl, but Tessa was still talking," Clark said with a thick layer of sarcasm on top.

Ronald jumped to his feet, nervously rubbing his sweater-clad stomach. People always said he looked like a panda bear and typically I didn't see that at all. But in this moment if I had squinted my eyes hard enough, the large belly and ever present dark under eye circles did resemble that of a panda bear.

As Ronald tried to chatter away and make peace between the two men, I quickly shot a glance at Mandy to try and figure out what was happening. I appeared to be the only one not in the loop.

"I'll tell you later," Mandy hissed. Well that wasn't much help, but I guess I would just have to wait. I slowly sat back down in my seat just as Clark looked ready to burst.

"Ronald, you can try to smooth this over as much as you want," Clark said. He was still speaking in a civil tone, but his voice kept getting louder and louder. "But no matter what, Earl is being greedy. We have always held the Hayride on your family's land and we still will."

"I know there isn't much I can do about it," Earl said. "But I can't promise that everything will go fine during the Hayride. Hopefully nothing happens to make it a bad experience. Goodness knows how much Shady Lake needs that money."

"Are you saying you would do

something to ruin the Halloween Hayride?" Clark said, his thick eyebrows knit together in confusion. "If you do, you will be in trouble. Mark my words."

I was a little bit shocked. In the few months I had known him, Clark was normally a very mild-mannered guy. Once we had been driving to dinner and someone had cut him off and he had shouted a bit, but that was about it. Apparently he didn't have road rage, but other people could push his buttons.

The hulking figure of Ralph shuffled slowly between Earl and Clark, looking quietly like he would pulverize Clark in an instant if need be. But Earl put a thin, bony hand on Ralph's forearm and pushed past him to shove himself into Clark's face.

"I hope you aren't threatening me, Clark," he said. "Ralph here doesn't take kindly to threats."

Ralph grunted and I had to suppress a giggle because this was almost too insane to be true. This was playing out like a scene in a badly acted movie, but instead of being curled up at home with a bowl of popcorn, I was sitting in a hard, vinyl chair with a cup of rapidly cooling coffee in front of me.

"No matter," Earl said. He waved his

hand flippantly. "You know what I am asking for. If I don't get it, you can kiss the Halloween Hayride goodbye."

Ralph eclipsed Earl from view and they both went out the front door of the Donut Hut. The tinkling of the bell was the only sound to cut the silence that was hanging around the committee. Clark stood seemingly frozen in time next to the table with his fingers still curling in and out of fists.

A scratching of pen on paper was the next thing to fill the silence. I looked over to see Chelsea furiously writing. The wheels in her head were probably already turning, trying to figure out how to write about this for tomorrow's paper. Everyone knew the deadline to get things printed was nine, so she was cutting it pretty close to get an article about this in.

"Miss Goodman, I would really appreciate it if you didn't print anything about this," Ronald said quietly. "The Tribune is not some lowly gossip rag. If anything, just post something about how the Hayride is coming together."

Chelsea sneered at Ronald and opened her mouth to spit back some sort of retort when Clark spoke up.

"Ronald is right," he said. "We can't let Earl get to us. The Halloween Hayride is going to happen and it is going to be our most profitable to date. If you write about the unsavory parts, people won't come out. Please don't write about it."

Clark gave her a sly smile. Chelsea set her pen down and slowly picked up the piece of paper. A small smile appeared on her face as she crumpled up the paper and threw it into the closest trash can.

"Whatever you say Clark," she said in a syrupy sweet voice.

Ronald sighed with relief as he rubbed his forehead with one hand. He stood at the head of the table once again and looked desperately at the agenda, trying to figure out where they were and what they should do next.

"Why don't we be done for the night," Mandy quietly suggested as she stood up from her chair. "We can reconvene another night and touch base on anything we didn't get to tonight. I think we hit all of the points we really needed to."

"That is a great idea, Mandy," Ronald said with a relieved smile on his face. "I will email you all tomorrow to set up our next meeting. Have a good night everyone."

I immediately grabbed a tray of donuts and headed to the kitchen. I had plans to eat one more seasonal pastry before I went home but Clark put his hand on my shoulder and gently took the tray out of my hands.

"Let me help you with that," he said with a sweet smile. His teeth were perfectly straight and his smile was so dazzling I loosened up my grip on the tray, totally forgetting the delicious, sugary sweetness I had been about to ingest. Instead I grabbed a carafe of coffee in each hand and led the way into the kitchen.

•Chapter 3•

As I packed up the leftover donuts into a box to take to the B&B as part of the breakfast the next morning, Mandy came in with a tray of dirty coffee cups. She started to load them into a dishwasher rack, but I just had to figure out exactly what had happened.

"Umm, so what is going on? Who is that guy that came in?"

"That is Earl Stone," Mandy said. I had gathered that bit, so I waved my hand to indicate I needed a little bit more to go on. Sometimes Mandy forgot that I hadn't lived in Shady Lake for close to a decade.

"The Hayride takes place on Earl's family land every year," Mandy said. "His uncle Gordon owned the used car dealership Stone Motors which, as you know, was the biggest financial supporter of the Hayride. He also let us use the land for free. But Gordon died last year and Earl took over both the dealership and the family land."

I remembered Gordon Stone. He was a lifelong bachelor who kept mostly to himself. He was a shy man who somehow was great at selling used cars, but couldn't manage to have a conversation about the weather. I think everyone shopped at his car lot because he gave a great deal without too much schmoozing. Plus, a lot of people felt bad for the old man who seemed lonely, but I think he was just an extreme introvert who liked his alone time.

"Earl's a little rat is what he is," Clark said as he poured the old coffee down the drain. "He came in here and not only is he running the dealership into the ground because he is so greedy, he keeps trying to charge us to use the land for the Hayride."

"Don't forget that he tried to pull the dealership's financial backing of the Hayride," Mandy said quietly. She wasn't one to spout off gossip, but she had no problem telling the facts of the case.

"Tried to pull it?" I asked. "What stopped him?"

"Popular opinion," Clark said. "After his plan got out, there were dozens of letters to the editor calling for people to boycott Stone Motors. People were furious. Obviously the rat fink had to weigh his options and figured the financial output for the Hayride would be less of a hit than an ongoing boycott of the dealership."

I nodded as I tried to remember how

many guests were at the B&B that night and determining if I could get away with eating one of the donuts still. Along with not being able to keep my mouth shut, I had a bad habit of stress-eating sugary filled snacks. Both my brain and my waistline hated it.

"So who is this Ralph guy?" I asked as I picked up a donut and took a bite. If there weren't enough donuts for breakfast, someone would just have to make do with a muffin instead.

"We don't really know," Mandy said. "He appeared in town with Earl and as you can see, he isn't much for words. In fact, he never goes anywhere without Earl so no one has been able to talk to him alone."

I grabbed the decaf carafe from Clark before he could pour it all out and I poured myself a cup instead. I loved coffee, but this late at night it had to be decaf or I'd be up all night. I was on the breakfast shift at the B&B, so I had to sleep before serving the guests their meal the next morning.

Mandy pushed her way backward through the swinging door to the seating area to do one last check for the night. Out of the corner of my eye, I saw Clark making his way closer to me. I set down my coffee cup just in time for him to put his arm around my waist and pulled me close to him.

"It's been too long since our last date," he said, his forehead pressed against mine. "Are you free tomorrow night?"

"For you? Anytime," I said, trying not to get too flustered.

"Good," he smiled at me. "I have an idea in mind about what we should do, but you have to promise to not laugh and to hear me out."

"Umm okay."

"I need to make sure everyone knows how to drive the tractor pulling the Hayride, right? Well, instead of the group class this weekend, I thought I could give you a little one on one driving lesson."

"So our date will be in a random corn field?" I asked. Clark looked a little shocked and started to backpedal. "I'm just kidding. I think that sounds wonderful."

"Good, I will pick you up after football practice tomorrow night."

I shut my eyes and smiled. Clark's hands were warm on my waist, even through my shirt. Suddenly, the swinging door was pushed open hard and Mandy came back in. Clark and I jumped apart. Mandy just caught my eye and smirked at me as she put the last few plates in the dishwashing rack.

"Okay folks, we are all clean out there," Mandy said. "Time to go home."

"Alright, I will pick you up tomorrow night Tessa," he said. "Have a good night Mandy."

"Good night Clark," Mandy said.

"Good night," I said with a little wave. I had to lean against the big metal table in the middle of the kitchen to support myself as Clark left. He is so handsome and I still can't imagine what he sees in me. But I was determined to have fun with him while he saw something in me that he liked.

Mandy cleared her throat and I looked up to see her waiting for me. She had already put on her jacket and had her purse over her arm. She was holding out my jacket and purse towards me. I looked at her blankly and she shook my stuff at me until I walked over to her.

"Time to go, lovebird," she said with the same smirk on her face.

"Don't give me that look," I said as I grabbed my things. I shoved my arms into my fleece jacket and zipped it up. Minnesota autumn is no joke and soon enough I'd have to switch over to my winter jacket.

"I'm not giving you a look," Mandy said, definitely still giving me a look. I know she just wants me to go slow when it comes to dating, but I don't know how to convince her that I'm fine. I am going slow. But she doesn't know what regular dating is like. She moved in with her fiance Trevor after only three days of dating. But my thoughts on Trevor are best kept for another night because I'm on Cloud Nine right now and Trevor just brings me down.

"Oh whatever, let's go," I said as I threw my purse strap over my head. I was a little annoyed, but Mandy and I had been friends for so long that we could almost read each other's minds.

I walked out the back door into the alley to the station wagon I drove now. Technically, it was my parent's car. But I used it to run errands for the B&B and motel that they own. My dad is a car guy. The shed behind our house has four old cars that my dad has been slowly working on. When everyone is over for Sunday dinner, our house looks like a used car dealership.

Mandy locked the alley door and shuffled over to the station wagon's passenger side.

She was meeting Trevor for dinner and I was going to drop her off so they only had one car there. As soon as she fell into the car, I hit the gas. Mandy was pushed back into her chair as she struggled to buckle her seatbelt.

"Geez, Tessa. What the heck?"

"Sorry Mandy."

The alley was almost pitch black besides one tiny light over the bakery back door and my headlights. But there were still a bunch of places that were just all shadows. Ever since Peter died, I found myself scared of the dark. On one hand, it feels ridiculous. I am thirty years old; I shouldn't need a night light. But my therapist assured me that I've been through a traumatic event and that being afraid of the dark is totally normal. I just hope I don't have to carry a flashlight in my purse for a long time because the heavy metal one I have really weighs my purse down.

•Chapter 4•

Snap snap

"Hello, is there anyone in there," a woman said, snapping her fingers in front of my face. She was a tall, willowy woman dressed in yoga pants and a sweater dress. I immediately pegged her as a suburban dweller, probably coming to enjoy the autumn leaves. They were my least favorite because they tended to be the most demanding. It was a little odd that she appeared to be alone, however. Usually the leaf peepers came in pairs.

I was sitting at the front desk of the B&B listening to my favorite podcast. Usually mid-morning on a Tuesday is pretty slow, so I put my headphones on and catch up on my favorites. I tend to get really into the true crime ones, which was always a bit appalling for Peter. He used to joke that I was studying up in case I decided to off him.

"I'm sorry ma'am," I said as I took my headphones off and hit pause on my podcast. "Are you checking in?"

"Obviously that is why I'm here," she snapped. "My name is Susy Martin. I called for a reservation yesterday."

I checked the computer registration and found her name. My dad had put in her information yesterday and, as usual, his forgetfulness meant he didn't tell me we had a new guest. Usually, my parents would alert me to new guests so I wouldn't be totally caught off guard when they showed up. Otherwise I had to deal with snobs being upset I wasn't just sitting at this table staring into space and waiting for them to arrive.

"Yes, here you are Ms. Martin," I said. I put together the folder of information we give to guests. Besides their key, we give a little menu with our weekly breakfasts, a list of activities going on in town that week, and places of interest they may want to visit by themselves. Susy impatiently tapped her foot and sighed a few times while she waited for me to finish.

"I don't really need all of that," she said as I started to explain what everything was.

"Oh, well why don't you just take the folder in case you need it," I suggested.

"Just give me my key and I'll be on my way," Susy snapped. She flapped her hands around as she spoke. "I'm only in town for a few days and I'm here for a very specific reason. I don't need to know about the Historical Museum or anything like that."

"Here you go, Ms. Martin," I said in my most syrupy sweet voice as I handed her the entire folder of information. I was biting my tongue so hard I was almost drawing blood. But I was determined not to run my parent's business into the ground just because I couldn't keep my mouth shut.

She snatched the folder out of my hand and walked towards the staircase. As she walked, she took the key out of the folder and dropped the rest of it on the floor. Thankfully she didn't turn around because I may or may not have shown a certain finger before I could stop myself. Then I slapped myself in the forehead because I really needed to stop letting my impulsive side get the best of me.

"Oh Tessa, what did you do this time?" my mother, Teri said as she walked in pulling the vacuum behind her. I have been impulsive my entire life and my poor mother has always been as supportive as possible.

"It was nothing Mom," I said. "Ms. Martin is just a little bit, umm, difficult to please. But I think we are all okay for now."

She crossed the room and gave me a big

hug. By this point in my life, she didn't have to ask about what I was feeling. She knew I hated how impulsive I could be and that I was always filled with regret afterwards. It was the one part of my personality that I would change if I could.

"Well I'm here now," my mom said. "I can keep an eye on the desk for a while if you want to go out and have a break."

"Thanks Mom," I said. I grabbed my phone and keys off of the desk and headed outside before my dad came around with a different job for me to do. I hopped in the station wagon and turned on the car. The radio was always tuned to 920 AM, Shady Lake's AM radio station. They played old country songs, church services, high school sports, and a long running segment called "Party Line" where people could call in and make any sort of announcement they wanted to make. Right now, a woman was describing the garage sale she was having at her house, making sure to include descriptions of many of the items that would be for sale. From the sounds of it, she had been talking for a while and Don, the longtime radio host, was trying to find a polite way to get her to wrap it up.

I quickly decided to go drown my

sorrows in a donut. All of the leftover donuts I brought home last night had been devoured before I could get one this morning. I had expected that, but I still was disappointed when the empty plate of crumbs came back to the kitchen.

My drive to the Donut Hut took me on Lake Road, which ran entirely around Shady Lake. The lake was ringed by a sidewalk and a row of beautiful trees with red and orange leaves. By this point in the year, everyone has taken their docks out of the water and we are left with a beautiful, clear view of the lake.

Sometimes when I drive around the lake, I wonder why I ever left for the big city. I already know the answer: Peter. I loved Peter and I followed him where he wanted to go. He had grown up in a suburb and wanted to be close to his friends. And I'm not going to lie and say I didn't like living up there. We had a great time trying out restaurants and bars.

But I feel so much more comfortable here in a small town. I know where everything is and I know who almost everyone is. As I drive, everyone waves and I wave back. It feels good to be back and snuggle back into the town that helped raised me.

I turned off of Lake Road onto Main Street. I stopped at a stop sign and looked over to see a man and a woman standing together next to a large, flashy, silver car. It was not the type of car we typically saw here in Shady Lake, so I was intensely curious about who was driving it.

I glanced around the intersection quickly to see I was the only one there. I started to roll through and squinted to try and recognize who was standing next to the fancy car. As I got closer, I saw the back of a woman's head with a large, blond hairdo that I didn't really recognize standing next to a short man who had his hand on her waist in what would be an intimate way if it wasn't grasping the woman. It looked like they might be in some sort of an argument.

But the male face glared at me, obviously recognizing me before I recognized him. I gasped as I realized that Earl was the man staring back at me. I tentatively gave a small wave, but hit the gas and got myself out of there. I pulled into a parking space in front of the Donut Hut and ran inside. I collapsed into a booth with a wave towards the counter.

Soon enough, Mandy slid into the other side of the booth while placing a plate in front of me. She had picked out a long john with green frosting and sprinkles that look like eyeballs. I must look terrible if she thought I needed this kind of seasonal pastry.

"Spill. Tell me what happened," she said after I devoured the first few bites.

"Well, I'm not sure it was a big deal," I said. "It was just kind of weird."

I described to her how I saw Earl next to the car with a woman and how he sneered at me as I tried to wave at him. Once I reached the end of the story, I took another large bite of donut. The sweetness was helping me overcome the weird anxiety that had hit earlier.

"First of all, that woman is Candy," Mandy said rolling her eyes. Candy had been a few years older than us in high school and Mandy had always been annoyed because their names rhymed and would sometimes be mixed around despite the fact that they were not at all alike and didn't even look alike. "Second of all, were you sure Ralph wasn't there? He is always with Earl."

"I'm pretty sure I would have noticed a giant third person standing with them," I said. "It was definitely just the two of them.

And I haven't heard much from Candy since high school. How did she get mixed up with Earl?"

"Hold on, I need a sweet treat also," Mandy said. She darted up to the counter and grabbed a second Halloween long john and two cups of coffee.

"Okay, so here's the deal," she said after a few bites. "Candy kind of disappeared after high school for like three years. But then she reappeared and she seemed to keep attaching herself to anyone who had a little money. She would date them for a while and then there would be some sort of drama and all of a sudden she would be on the arm of someone else."

"You're just saying that because you never liked her in high school," I pointed out.

"True, but I did try to befriend her when she came back," Mandy said. "Candy came in here and asked if I was hiring. I was, so I gave her an application. I tried to start some small talk and ask her how life was going. I must have asked too many questions because she got really annoyed and ended up shoving the paper back at me. She told me she didn't want to work here anyways."

My eyebrows knit together in confusion. I

do know Candy had grown up without a lot of money. I wonder why she would come in for a job and leave without even applying. And how did she find Earl now? And what in the world did she see in Earl?

As I took the last sip of my coffee, I glanced at the clock to see it was already late afternoon. Clark would be by to pick me up in less than an hour, so I needed to get home and get ready. Even if our date was in cornfield, I still wanted to look good.

•Chapter 5•

Whenever I had a date, I always made sure I was ready way early. The idea of not being ready when the guy got here gave me an anxious stomachache, so when I got home I quickly changed clothes into a cute flannel shirt and jeans with a vest over it to keep me warm. Deep down inside, I hoped that Clark would keep me warm.

I sat in the bay window thumbing through a magazine that was on the side table. I used to be attached to my phone and would have been scrolling social media or playing some dumb game. But when I moved back to Shady Lake, I decided that I wanted to break my smart phone addiction. Now, I have a flip phone. The first time I took it out around Mandy, she almost fell on the floor laughing. But I think she spends too much time on social media.

"Hey sweetie, where are you headed?" My dad plopped into the other chair in the bay window. From the looks of it, he had been tasked with dusting. While his salt and pepper hair was now more salt than pepper, some of that was definitely dust and cobwebs.

"Clark is taking me out to practice driving the tractor for the hayride," I said. I purposely didn't look at my dad because he tends to still think of me as Daddy's little girl, even though I've already been married once. But out of the corner of my eye, I could see him shake his head a little bit.

"Well that will be an exciting night," he said. "Do you think you'll be able to handle driving that big ole tractor?"

"Of course I can," I said. "Besides, it is better I learn now instead of during the Hayride."

"Sure, sure," my dad said. He liked to rib me and I was about the only person he would tolerate to dish it right back to him. But I wasn't going to get into it with him tonight.

I saw Clark's truck pull up outside. He got out of the truck and headed towards the door. I hurried up and gave my dad a hug, ignoring the scowl on his face. He wasn't a big Clark fan except for his work as a football coach. Dating his daughter was a different story.

I opened the front door just as Clark lifted his hand to knock. We both did the awkward laugh thing as Clark shuffled his feet a little bit. I grabbed my purse off of the entryway table.

"Well, let's go," I said, shutting the door behind me before my dad could say anything to him. Clark offered his arm and I put my hand in the crook of his elbow. Together, we walked to the truck where Clark opened the passenger side door for me. His pickup truck sat high up off of the ground and Clark offered me his hand. I gratefully accepted as I climbed up and in.

Clark took off down the driveway and as we pulled away, I saw my dad still standing in the bay window. I waved my hand and he waved back, which was a good sign that he wasn't actually upset with me.

The field where the Hayride was held was a good fifteen minutes away, so we had a little time to talk. It was actually so far that instead of making the townspeople drive to the field and back, we set up a bus system from the high school parking lot. It cut down on figuring out where to park everybody and having to worry about people getting lost out in the country looking for the place.

"So, I have something I've been curious about for a while," Clark said. I froze for a moment, wondering if he was going to ask about Peter. While I enjoyed talking about him to my family and Mandy, I was definitely not ready to talk about my first husband with a man I was out on a date with. I tried to take a few deep breaths as it felt like I'd just drank a large glass of ice water.

"How come you live in a bed and breakfast?" he asked. "That seems kind of weird and potentially awkward."

I must have been holding my breath because suddenly I exhaled out a laugh. It was a weird, throaty laugh that was much different from my normal laugh, but Clark didn't seem to notice.

"It can be kind of weird," I admitted. This was a question I could deal with. "But my parents have owned the Shady Lake Motel for a long time so they are used to the hospitality field. When we were younger, my parents bought a giant house because there are five of us kids. Once we all moved out, they decided they wanted to keep the house but they didn't want it empty. Interestingly enough, in the state of Minnesota, the owners of a bed and breakfast have to live on site."

"Really?" Clark said. He seemed genuinely interested in what I had to say in a decidedly boring conversation. We turned from a paved city street onto a gravel road that led out of town.

"Yeah, so they decided that would be the best way to enjoy their house," I said. "They renovated so that we have our own private family space upstairs. Of course, they didn't expect their thirty year old daughter to move in, but it has been nice to be able to help them out."

"I'm sure they are glad you moved back," Clark said. "I'm sure glad you did otherwise I never would have met you."

Clark took my hand and gave it a squeeze. I'm not sure if he knows much about why I moved back, but he sure was sweet. I realized I was making goo-goo eyes at him, but I just couldn't help myself.

"We are almost there, but since we are trapped in this truck a little longer, now I have another question," Clark said. "Don't worry. This one is a bit more exciting. I was kinda wondering if maybe you wanted to coordinate our Halloween costumes? You know, like do a couples costume?"

"Oh that would be so fun," I blurted out. "Like being ketchup and mustard or something?"

"I was thinking more like a cowboy and cowgirl or something," Clark laughed. I immediately felt my face get warm. Why did I have to open my big, dumb mouth sometimes?

"Yeah, that sounds good too," I mumbled as I turned to look out the window. Clark squeezed my hand again and when I glanced at him, a smile spread across his face. I smiled back at him, feeling a little less stupid.

We turned down a gravel driveway that led into a field. There were a few sheds around the property that used to hold farming equipment, but over the years had turned into storage for the Hayride. Clark pulled the truck up in front of one of the sheds and shifted into park.

I hopped out of the cab and Clark got out to open up the shed doors. This was the shed where the big rusty tractor was stored. It wasn't pretty to look at, especially after it had been painted orange to try and go with the Halloween theme. But it ran like a dream.

Clark shoved the door open, but the shed was empty. Instead of a hard to miss orange tractor, there was just a large empty space inside.

"What the…" Clark said as he took a step back. I glanced around at the other sheds, wondering if any of them were big enough to house an entire tractor. Maybe it was just in a different shed for some reason.

"Could it be in that shed over there?" I asked, pointing to the only other large enough shed on the property. All of the other ones were just little concession stands or only big enough to house a few little tables in case of inclement weather during the Hayride.

"I suppose it could be," Clark shrugged. I got the feeling he and I were in agreement that whoever took out the tractor last time maybe shouldn't be allowed to drive it again. It seemed like forgetting where you are supposed to put the tractor means automatic tractor banishment.

We started walking towards the other large shed on the property when I caught a glimpse of orange out of the corner of my eye. The tractor was sitting in the middle of the field, seemingly abandoned.

"Hey," I said, tugging on Clark's sleeve. "I found the tractor."

"What in the world is it doing out there?" he seemingly asked to the sky as I also had no idea why it was there. "I wonder if maybe someone took it out and it ran out of gas? Maybe they just didn't know what else to do with it."

I followed Clark as we tromped through the field towards the tractor when suddenly he stopped short and I ran straight into the back of him. Thankfully I was directly behind him otherwise I would have taken an elbow to the face.

"Hey, what's the big deal?" I asked. Clark turned around, his face looking pale. He looked like he'd just seen a ghost.

"I don't think you'll want to see this," he said. For a second, I thought he might be playing a joke on me. But then I peered around him.

Lying on the ground behind the tractor was a large lump that looked like a piece of roadkill. But this wasn't just an unlucky raccoon or rabbit. Earl Stone had been run over by the Halloween Hayride.

•Chapter 6•

The flashing red and blue lights lit up the hayride field and made it really feel like Halloween. After we called the emergency line, Clark and I had sat in his truck, quietly listening to the radio and waiting for the police to come. It was a completely surreal scene and I know for sure that I didn't really know what to say. Apparently Clark hadn't either, because besides the polka hour that played on 920 AM, it had been silence until the first squad car appeared on the scene. When the driver's side door swung open, I let out a quiet squeak. It must not have been quiet enough though because Clark looked at me like I was crazy until he also noticed who had gotten out of the police car.

I love Shady Lake, but the one thing I hate about small towns is how the people you don't want to see always end up right where you are. The first officer on the scene was Officer Max Marcus aka my high school boyfriend aka the other guy I have been casually seeing since I moved back to town. He also happened to be the exact physical opposite of Clark. Where Clark had dark hair and was tall and thin, Max was blond haired and blue eyed. He was short and stocky, but in a way where he had plenty of muscle on his body.

The biggest thing was that where Clark and I had just met a few months ago, Max and I had met in elementary school and dated for almost six years. We got together in junior high and stayed together all through high school. We were that couple that everyone thought would last forever.

Except I decided to move away to go to college and Max didn't. A long distance relationship just didn't work for us once I met Peter. It didn't help that Max met someone else too. But here we were now. Ten years later and we were dating again. Unfortunately, one of the things we have in common now is the fact that we were both recently widowed.

Max smiled at me as he walked up to the truck and then noticed that Clark was in the driver's seat. His smile quickly changed into a scowl. Now before you think I was two timing either of these men, rest assured that Max and Clark definitely know about each other. They both know that I date both of them. They both go out and date other women also. None of the three of us is in a place in life where we want to be exclusively dating anyone. But that doesn't mean they necessarily like each other. The one thing they have in common is that they are both very competitive, especially when it comes to me.

I opened the truck door and hopped down onto the gravel driveway. I waved a little at Max as I shut the truck door. Max had already recovered from seeing Clark and I together and now he was all business.

"Hey there Tessa," he said. "I need you and Clark to show me what happened here."

"Sure, come on over here Max," Clark said. He started towards the tractor with Max close on his heels. I trailed behind, watching the ground as I walked. I watched a lot of crime shows and I know that sometimes people bumble around crime scenes with no regard to the state of any potential clues. I was determined not to do that. Plus, I just didn't really want to step in something gross.

When I caught up to the men, they were looking back and forth between the tractor and Earl's body. This time, I got a better look at the body and it was pretty obvious that he had been run over by the tractor. I wandered over to get a closer look at the tractor.

"Do you think he was trying to drive the tractor and fell over the front and got run over?" Clark asked. The undertone of his question was that obviously Earl probably didn't know how to drive a tractor. He seemed like a city slicker.

"That doesn't seem likely," I chimed in. "First of all, falling over the front would be pretty hard. Second of all, look at the tractor. Whoever was driving was wearing denim jeans. And Earl is definitely in a pair of khakis."

"You're right," Max said. I could see the wheels turning in his head. Obviously he had been under the impression that whatever had happened had been an accident. But that seemed to have flipped with the discovery of the denim threads. Plus it wasn't like Earl Stone was some beloved town figure who everyone loved.

"I'm going to walk you two back to your truck to wait," Max said. "And I'm sorry, but I'll need you to give me your keys so I know you won't be able to go anywhere. I know we will have more questions for you but we need to investigate a little bit first."

"That seems a bit much," Clark said. He

was clutching his truck keys tight in his fist as his eyes flashed. It didn't take much of a challenge from Max to get him fired up.

"Well maybe I need to detain you in my squad car seeing as you were the first person on the scene, you are wearing denim jeans, and you've previously had a run-in with the deceased," Max said. He had to actually look up to look Clark in the face, but he puffed his chest out to make up for it.

"Oh for goodness sake, can you both relax a bit," I said. It seemed like an odd thing to say at the scene of a potential murder, but so was having a duel over my love at a crime scene. "Clark, it makes sense that the police don't want us to leave as we were the ones who discovered the body. Max, Clark obviously didn't kill Earl. He went straight from football practice to picking me up for our date. Plus, he doesn't have any pieces missing from his pants."

They both managed to scowl at me before nodding their agreement. By this point, an ambulance and three more police cars had pulled up and the officers had been taking pictures and taping off the crime scene so no one else could get into the field.

Clark and I walked back and sat in the

bed of his truck. There was no use climbing in the front of the truck. We didn't have the keys, so it wasn't like we could listen to music or anything. At least it was still somewhat warm outside so we didn't have to worry about getting cold. Plus we could see more of what the police officers were doing from the truck bed.

I really didn't have to worry about getting cold because as soon as we were both sitting on the tailgate, Clark pulled me as close as he could and put his arm around me. I did a quick scan of my surroundings and saw that Max wasn't anywhere in sight, so I relaxed into the side of him.

"Well this is a heck of a date," Clark said. "I know you like Halloween, but this is a bit much."

"Yeah, unfortunately this is just how things go in my life," I sighed. "Not that I stumble across dead bodies all the time. Just that things never really go how I plan them. I've ended up in strange situations way more times than I can count."

Clark chuckled and rubbed his hand up and down my flannel clad arm. The warmth exploded through my entire body. I knew I could count on him to help warm me up.

"But what do you think happened to

Earl?" I asked. I was so curious. This was just like one of my podcasts coming to life. I think sometimes that I watch too many crime shows for my own good. But maybe not considering what had happened.

"Who cares?" Clark scoffed. "It isn't like it's a giant loss to our community. At least now he won't be ruining the Halloween Hayride."

"Really?" I asked. "Because I think he kind of already did. Just not in the way that he was expecting to."

No matter what happened, I decided in that moment that I needed to make sure that the Halloween Hayride would still go on as planned.

•Chapter 7•

Clark was in the back of a squad car giving a statement. They had taken me over first, but I didn't have a lot to say because I hadn't actually discovered the body. I had been too busy running into Clark's back. They were more interested in what Clark saw when he first stumbled upon Earl.

So I took advantage of the fact that Clark would be a while and decided to try to do some snooping of my own. Besides, I was stuck out in that field with no way home and not even a radio to listen to. I needed something to do. I rationalized that I listened to a lot of true crime stuff, so I knew the basic things you shouldn't do at a crime scene.

I tried to look as casual as possible but even though I stuck out like a sore thumb as one of the only people there not in a uniform, somehow I managed to walk right on by everyone. I tried to look sharp just in case I spotted a clue. But mostly I just saw the old sheds and a bunch of grass and trees.

The police had used the yellow tape to mark off a giant area around the tractor and

Earl's body. That meant that even if I did find anything, it probably wouldn't be relevant to the case. I sat down at one of the tables in the dining shed and looked at my phone. Of course, no one had called or texted me and I didn't have any apps I could check. So I flipped it shut and jammed it back into my pocket.

"What do you think you are doing?" a voice boomed from the shadows.

I jumped to my feet immediately. My adrenaline was racing and I tried to calculate which exit was the closest for me to get out of the shed. I turned to face the voice, sure it had to be the murderer. Instead, Max was grinning at me as he stepped closer to me.

"Max, you scared the living daylights out of me," I said. "I was sure I was going to be the next one murdered."

"I didn't mean to scare you Sweet Thing," he said, using his old high school nickname for me. Every time I heard him call me that, I became a puddle. I'm pretty sure he knew that too, which was why he used it so often. "But I do know that you are definitely not supposed to be over here. I need you to wait by the truck until your date can take you home."

"I just got so bored," I said. "Can't we have the keys now? I was already interviewed and Clark is talking to the other cops now. I just want to listen to the radio."

Max thought about it for a second and then dug the keys out of his pocket. He turned them over in his his hands a few times before flipping them to me with a low toss. I barely managed to catch them.

"I supposed that's alright," he said. "But hey Tessa? Don't go snooping around. You haven't changed much since high school and I remember how much you liked to play detective back then."

I blushed a bit, remembering how I used to try to help girls who thought their boyfriends were two-timing them. I would set up entire reconnaissance missions to try and catch them in a lie. And you know what? I was darn good at it. That has been the start of my true crime obsession, I think.

I watched Max walk away from me back to the crime scene. He was definitely a man who looked good in a uniform. I started back towards the truck when I realized the keyring had a small flashlight on it. I turned it on and scanned the ground. It had been an exciting enough night; I didn't need to make it any more exciting by breaking my ankle.

Looking down, I spotted a large boot print in the dirt. It was a little odd considering it looked like the print of a heavy duty boot someone would wear once it snowed. It was probably just Max's police boot. But then I noticed that the boot prints from where Max had been standing were a totally different print.

I started to follow the boot prints. There were a few, one right after the other. It looked like whoever made these prints had been in the field by the tractor and had walked towards the sheds and gravel driveway.

One glance back towards the squad car with Clark in it confirmed that he was still giving his story. I definitely wanted to follow these boot prints. I had an insatiable appetite, so the same thing that made me binge listen to murder podcasts also urged me to follow these footprints

The prints were pretty far apart, almost as if this person with the large, heavy-duty boots had been running. Maybe they had been running for help after an accident with the tractor? Or maybe they had been running away from a person they had just murdered?

When I followed the prints to the yellow tape, I bowed under it and kept following. I tried to walk down low to the ground to try not to attract attention to myself.

"I told you that you needed to leave the area," Max's voice boomed again. I snapped my head up and saw Max charging in my direction. Crap, definitely not what I wanted to happen.

"Tessa, what the heck," Max said quietly as he got close to me. He was trying to remain ever the professional law enforcement officer, but also didn't want to make me angry. "I told you to stop. Just let us handle it."

"Sorry Max," I said. "But I was just looking at these boot prints that seem to be coming from the crime scene. I was wondering if you had seen them and if they could be a clue."

Max looked down and I couldn't quite tell, but he seemed to get a little pale. He squatted down to get a better look and after a beat, I did too. I wanted a closer look at them. Plus I didn't need another cop to see me inside the tape and come over to yell at me. Max was mumbling to himself.

"Do you think it is a clue?" I asked. I could tell there was just a touch too much excitement in my voice, but I couldn't help it. I was investigating a real crime scene.

"It might be," Max said. "I can't believe I missed this."

He stood up and waved another officer over. A younger man jogged over and Max told him to stand guard over the footprints while he walked me back to the truck. He grabbed me by the elbow and gently started to walk towards the truck. I stole a glance at his face and could tell that he was annoyed. It was well hidden, but after you date someone for so long, you can read the more subtle expressions on their face.

"I'm sorry Max," I said. "I didn't mean to mess things up."

"Well, I'd actually say it was more of a help than messing things up," Max said. "It is kind of annoying that I missed it in the first place. But don't take that as a sign that you should snoop around any more. So thanks, but now I really want you to go."

"Are you mad at me?" I asked quietly.

"Kind of," he said. "But there is one thing you can do to make me feel a little better."

I thought about that for a moment. Technically I was on a date with another guy, so I wasn't going to kiss him or anything. But I took the bait and asked.

"What can I do?" I asked.

"You can dress up for Halloween with me," he said. "And we can go together to the Halloween Hayride."

I tried not to look too shocked. I had already agreed to dress up with Clark. But one look at Max's hopeful face and the knowledge that he was upset with me was just too much.

"Okay sure," I blurted out. "That sounds fun."

Max's face broke into a wide, toothy smile. He ran his hand through his blond hair, which was always a sign that he was unabashedly happy. Well I was glad he was happy, because I had just walked myself into a real pickle. All of a sudden, I was supposed to be in a couples costume with two different men. And I was pretty sure they wouldn't agree for it to be a trio costume instead.

So now I had two mysteries to solve: Who killed Earl? And who would I end up in a couples costume with?

•Chapter 8•

Clink

I startled at the sudden sound of Mandy setting down a ceramic cup of coffee on the table in front of where I was currently resting my head on my arms. After finally leaving the field, Clark had dropped me off at home. But my parents were waiting up for me. They had heard all of the sirens and turned on the police scanner to hear all of the details. They had tried to call me, but of course my flip phone had been shoved down in my pocket while I was doing my investigation.

Instead, I had spent almost two hours talking to my parents once I was home. I had gone over every detail from how we found Earl's body to which police officers had shown up. Part of it was morbid curiosity on their part, which was definitely an integral part of living in a small town. Part of it was my need to go over all of the details. And part of it was figuring out exactly what to tell any guests who may catch wind of the murder. Thankfully, most people who stayed at the inn were originally from Shady Lake and probably wouldn't be scared off. And most of the motel guests were only around for a night or two before moving on.

So here I was the next morning slurping down coffee to try and wake up. I had been so exhausted that I had forgotten to turn off my alarm for the next morning. Once I woke up at 6, I hadn't been able to go back to sleep. My parents had nicely suggested that instead of bumbling around trying to serve breakfast, maybe I should head down the the Donut Hut for some coffee and breakfast.

"Once you are done gulping down that coffee, I'd really like to hear about what in the world happened last night," Mandy said. I had sent her a text when I got home and was half asleep last night that said I had found a dead body so naturally she wanted to hear a few more details.

"I gather it was connected to all of that police stuff happening down by the field," Mandy said. I knew that she knew more than she was letting on. She had an annoying habit of trying to get information by acting innocent and clueless except she was chewing her lip which was always a dead giveaway. Plus Trevor worked as a dispatcher, so even if he hadn't been on duty last night, one of his buddies would have alerted him to the unique situation.

"Okay, it isn't really that exciting of a story," I began.

"Umm, earth to Tessa, you found a dead body," Mandy jumped in, almost jumping out of her chair with excitement. "Of course it was exciting! So spill."

And spill I did, telling her every detail and ending with the problem of who I would decide to plan a costume with. By the time I got to the end, Mandy's eyes were gigantic, almost popping out of her head. She had been excitedly drinking coffee the entire time I had been talking.

"So who are you going to dress up with? Clark or Max?" Mandy asked. She was wringing her hands in front of her, in obvious distress for my situation. She and Trevor had been dating for a long time and despite my dislike for him, they never really fought. So my love life struggles were now her soap opera. That was just fine because her excitement meant she was more than willing to also help me figure out the messes I get myself into.

"I have no idea, but I'm more concerned with making sure the Halloween Hayride happens as scheduled," I said.

"Well you don't really have to worry too much because I have news too," Mandy said. She folded her hands and leaned across the table conspiratorially. "Trevor says that they already have a prime suspect."

Now it was my turn for my eyes to pop out. How in the world did they have a suspect already? Maybe I really was a crappy detective if I hadn't already figured it out. I pushed my self-doubt aside and waited for Mandy to spill the beans. She was drawing out the conversation by slowly eating her donut and drinking her coffee. I may have been the one to move away to the big city for a while, but Mandy had no trouble bringing drama on her own.

"The police are thinking Ralph may have done it," she whispered across the table at me. "You know, that big oaf who always follows Earl around?"

"That would certainly make sense considering the big footprint I found," I said. I leaned back in my chair to think a little more about it. I realized I didn't know all that much about Ralph or Earl. I'd need to put on my investigative hat and snoop around a bit. I did feel a little guilty because Max had distinctly told me not to investigate. But it wasn't just every day that a real life murder mystery falls into my lap.

Ding ding

The door opened and Ronald walked in looking dazed. That poor man always seemed to take the weight of the world onto his shoulders. Or, at least, the weight of Shady Lake. He stood in the doorway for a moment before he spotted me. A few of the other regulars tried to wave and greet him, but he seemed not to notice them. He smiled briefly at me as he started to make his way over.

"I really should get back to work," Mandy said. "I'll leave you to deal with Mayor Panda."

I grabbed her arm to stop her as she tried to walk past me to the kitchen.

"Hey, are you busy tonight?" I asked. "Because I have a few things I need to do and I need a partner in crime."

"You're lucky I'm free, bored, and Trevor is working," Mandy said. "Because I'm a little afraid you mean that literally."

"I'll pick you up at 7," I whispered. Mandy winked at me and went back to work.

As Ronald lumbered up to my table, I noticed he looked even worse close up. His shirt which was usually crisply ironed, was all wrinkled. The black circles under his eyes were even more pronounced than usual. His shirt had even been buttoned wrong. He didn't even bother to smile again as he waved to a few of the townspeople that he walked by. Apparently he had been on a mission to find me and once he did, he could greet other people.

"Tessa, I'm sure you've heard what happened," he said gravely as he sat down across from me. He folded his hands in front of him on the table. "If not, I come bearing some very bad news."

"Don't worry Mayor," I said. "I know all about what happened last night. I was actually there when the body was discovered."

Ronald's mouth gaped open and I gathered that he had not been told much about what had happened. I thought it was awfully strange for the mayor to not know what was going on.

"Oh I'm so sorry to hear that Tessa," Ronald said. "What an awful thing to have happen. I was not aware you had been there. But I was glad to see you. We are going to need some good planning to make sure this Hayride happens and is just as profitable as it is other years."

"Don't worry Mayor," I said. "I will make it my personal mission to make sure that this Hayride is successful. Whatever happened to Earl can't change one of Shady Lake's oldest and most fun traditions."

Ronald looked visibly relieved, letting out a large exhale as he sat back in his chair. I almost wanted to get up and give him a big hug, but I settled instead for a friendly little pat on his forearm. Suddenly, I noticed that the special watch Ronald always wore was gone. All employees of the city were given a special watch once they had been working there for five years. It was a source of pride for all employees and once they received them, they wore them proudly.

"Is your watch being repaired?" I asked. "I don't think I've ever seen you not wearing it."

Ronald stared at his wrist as if he had just noticed it was gone. The wrist he normally wore it on even had a small indent where it always sat. But today Ronald absentmindedly rubbed the indent while he stared off into the distance.

"I'm actually not sure where it is," he said. "I just noticed it was gone when you pointed it out. I'm actually going to leave you now so I can figure out what I did with it."

He rose from his chair and started to make his way to the door. He walked almost as if he were in a daze.

"Ronald," I called. He turned and looked at me. "I promise I will make sure that the Hayride happens."

"Thank you Tessa," he said. Ronald smiled a real, genuine smile. "I appreciate that."

And I meant it. I was going to get to the bottom of this murder. No one could come to Shady Lake and just ruin our Halloween Hayride.

•Chapter 9•

At seven o'clock sharp,I pulled up in front of Mandy's building. She lived above the Donut Hut downtown. When her parents owned the Donut Hut, they used to rent out the apartment upstairs for a little extra income. When Mandy took over, she decided to just move in because she and Trevor needed a place to live anyways.

I parked in the alley next to the shop like I normally did. I wasn't supposed to, but I did it anyways. Mandy came bounding out of the door, dressed in head to toe black. Sometimes I swore that we were mindlinked. All I had told her was that we were going to go do some things and she had rightly assumed that meant some shady investigation that required stealth. I was also dressed all in black and had brought along a bag of dark clothes for Mandy, which would apparently not be needed.

Mandy jumped in the front seat of the station wagon. Her eyes were dancing with excitement. She might say she doesn't like gossip or to meddle, but she had no qualms joining my meddling.

"Where are we headed?" she asked. "I'm

assuming the field?"

"You bet your sweet bippy," I said as I shifted into drive and rolled out of the alleyway. I didn't like to park there at night and I was always glad when I was able to leave the alley.

The streetlights were coming on and as we drove by the high school, the soccer team was playing a game under the stadium lights. The stands were filled with spectators and I could even see the cheerleaders waving their red and blue pompoms. Even after a murder, Shady Lake still managed to be cozy and comforting. I turned onto a gravel road and drove out to the middle of nowhere.

"What are we going to do if there is a police officer stationed there?" Mandy asked over the low din of an old country western song on the AM station. "Won't it look awfully suspicious if we roll up all dressed in black?"

"Do you really think they have someone stationed out here?" I asked. "If they have a suspect already, I'm sure they think it is all cut and dry. But I'm not so sure it is."

"Why not?" Mandy asked. She was digging through her purse. She fished out a pack of gum and I stuck out my hand for a piece. She took out two pieces, one for each of us and she handed me a foiled wrapped piece.

"I just don't think Ralph makes sense as a suspect," I said. The headlights lit up just a small patch of gravel in front of my car as we drove. "I assume he is being paid by Earl, right? So why would he kill his source of income? And it seems like Ralph is the only person Earl wasn't a total jerk to. So what would be Ralph's motive?"

Mandy popped her gum for a few moments while she thought about it. It was a totally unappealing habit she had done since middle school, but the one upside to it was that it meant she was always carrying at least one pack of gum.

"You're right," she said with a shrug. "Once you actually think about it, it doesn't make much sense at all."

I nodded and slowed the car down. I always forgot where the actual turn-in for the field was. Plus, as we came up to the turn, I wanted to make sure we didn't look too suspicious just in case Mandy was right and there was someone there. But the coast was clear and I drove down and parked in front of the sheds.

"Here's our game plan," I said as I

handed Mandy a flashlight. "We are just going to walk slowly around the area and look for anything I missed before. But it is very important that we don't touch anything."

Mandy rolled her eyes at me, which I ignored. It's not that I think she's an idiot, but people mess up crime scenes all the time. I had to make sure she understood what to do. We both quietly climbed out of the car. I started to walk towards the field and I motioned for her to stay close to me.

We walked up the gravel driveway towards the field where the tractor was still sitting surrounded by tape. I swept my beam of light back and forth, looking for anything out of place. So far, all that I saw were a bunch of footprints that seemed to belong to the police. From the looks of it, they weren't too careful about where they walked. No wonder they had already bumbled when I had been the one to find the footprints.

When we got to the edge of the field, Mandy suddenly stopped. I turned back towards her and saw her clenching her jaw for a moment before the gum popping started up again, this time even more fast and furious than it had been before.

"You don't have to be scared," I said. "I'm pretty sure this wasn't just some random killing. The murderer won't be here any more."

"I know, I know," she said shaking her head violently. "I just can't get the thought out of my mind. Let's just finish up and get out of here."

I ducked under the caution tape and waited for Mandy to do the same. After a moment's hesitation, she did, all while muttering about why in the world she was friends with me at all. I ignored her and soldiered on into the field.

The ground was lumpy and grass covered. Even though it was a farm field, nothing had been farmed there in decades. It had been kept an empty field just for the Halloween Hayride. Someone came out once every two weeks and mowed it all down to the ground to keep it from becoming too overgrown. There were a few trees here and there and a giant rock in the middle of the field. It all made the large orange tractor stick out like a sore thumb.

"Hey, what's that?" Mandy said, suddenly stopping in her tracks.

I followed the beam of light coming from her flashlight, my eyes landing on something that was glinting in the light. I couldn't tell what it was or even how big it was.

"I'm not sure," I said. "Stay here and keep your light on it and I'll go over and check it out."

I tried not to get too hopeful that I'd found some big clue because most likely, we had found something like a gum wrapper left over from the last Halloween Hayride. But as I got closer, I realized it was much bigger than a piece of garbage.

Holy moly, I thought. *I have hit the motherlode.*

Laying in the dirt, mostly covered by some weeds, was a watch. And not just any watch. It was a five year, commemorative watch. Just like the one that was given to all city employees. Just like the one Ronald had misplaced.

"Mandy, you're gonna want to see this," I called back to her. She tiptoed closer. She was going so slowly I just knew that she was unsure if I was gonna show her a clue or some severed body part. But when she got close enough, she gasped.

"No way," she said as she bent down to get a closer look. "Isn't that one of those fancy, city hall watches?"

"It certainly is," I said. "And Mayor Ronald was missing his watch when I talked to him this morning. When I asked him about it, he said he didn't know where it was."

Mandy stood up stick straight, seemingly frozen in time except for her eye which were darting back and forth. I took Mandy's phone out of her other hand and took a picture of exactly where the watch was and what it looked like when we found it. Then I used a stick to move it around and try to see it a little better. No doubt about it. It was definitely the watch of a city employee.

"But, you don't think Ronald could have done this, right?" she asked. I tried to answer, but I really didn't know. So I just opened and shut my mouth a few times, trying to think through exactly what I thought.

On one hand, Ronald certainly had a motive. Earl was trying to ruin the town's largest fundraiser. Ronald took his job as mayor very seriously. He wouldn't just let Earl get away with it. I'm sure whatever Earl had been doing out here that night hadn't been something to help us out. On the other hand, as far as I know, Ronald wouldn't hurt a fly. He was the nicest man ever. Plus, he would never put the Halloween Hayride at risk.

My mind was racing a million miles a minute. What should I do about the watch? I could call Max and tell him about it, except he explicitly told me not to come investigate. But I didn't want to leave it out here because there had to be another explanation.

"Mandy, go to my car and grab some tissues," I said, making my mind up. I wasn't one to mess up a crime scene, but I just couldn't imagine that Ronald had done this.

Mandy came back with a whole hand full of tissues. I carefully used one to pick up the watch and wrapped it up in a wad. If I needed to, I could turn this in later. But for now, I wanted to hold onto it until I got more information.

•Chapter 10•

I successfully hid the watch in the glove compartment of my car. I didn't want to risk touching it or having someone find it, so that seemed the best place to put it. Mandy and I swore each other to secrecy. We've kept many secrets together, but a potential clue in a murder investigation was a new one for us.

The next morning, I got a text message from Max as I was cleaning up the breakfast dishes. I washed the last couple of plates and dried my hands on the dish towel we always hung below the sink.

Hey, want to meet up for lunch?

The pit of my stomach started to feel all gurgly. Did he know about the watch? But there was no way he could know about what Mandy and I had done. Obviously the timing of his message was just a strange coincidence. I decided lunch would be okay. I headed into the dining room as I answered.

Sure, we can meet at the Taco Queen. See you at noon.

As I put my phone back in my apron, Susy rounded the corner. I startled a little bit and realized this was the first time I'd seen her since she had checked in. Even her car had been gone most of the time.

"Hello Ms. Martin," I said as I finished wiping the table. "How are you today?"

"I am doing much better than I was before," she replied. Considering my first interaction with her, she did seem a lot better. There was even a hint of a smile on her face. "I had some sad, but also wonderful news."

"Oh?" I said innocently. I had an idea of where this was going. "And what was that?"

Susy narrowed her eyes at me. I knew I was being a bit bold, but I didn't really care. Who has sad and wonderful news all at the same time? Besides, I had a hunch she might have known Earl.

"A distant relative died," she said. "But his death means I have inherited some land."

Ah-ha, so I was right, I thought.

"Were you related to Earl Stone by chance?" I asked before I could stop myself. The words just came tumbling out of my mouth. For a moment, Susy just stared at me.

"Yes, in fact I am," she said with a sneer.

"Or should I say I was. I actually came to talk to him about the land and the business. I didn't like what he was doing with either of them and I wanted to try and buy them from him. That little fink just wanted to rub them in my face, so he refused to sell. And then all of a sudden he was dead. Talk about fortuitous timing for me."

"So it seems like his death benefited you," I said. Once again, I regretted it as soon as the words left my mouth. Why was I such an idiot sometimes? But if I had gotten this far in life just letting my mouth spill out words before I thought about it, I was pretty sure I wasn't going to learn any time soon.

Susy opened her mouth for a moment, looking like she was about to scream at me. Then suddenly her eyes got wide and she ran out of the room, covering her mouth with one hand. I wasn't really sure what happened, but if it stopped me from being yelled at, I guess that was good.

Later that morning, I was just doing a final sweep of the main floor to make sure everything was where it was supposed to be before I left to meet Max for lunch. I heard a car start in the driveway, so I peeked out to see which guest was leaving.

Susy Martin's SUV was just pulling down

the driveway. And for someone who seemed so suburban, it was curiously dirty. It was almost as if it had been out in the country on some dirt roads.

Could she have something to do with Earl's murder? She certainly had motive. But then where had the giant footprint come from? And would a city girl like her even know how to drive a tractor? I filed all of that information away to think about another day. If I didn't get a move on, I was going to be late for my lunch date.

When I pulled up in front of the Taco Queen, I could see the squad car already parked out front. When I walked inside, Max was already at our usual table and my lunch was waiting for me. We had spent many, many of our high school lunchtimes at that very table and it was nice to be able to rely on the familiarity when I was with Max.

The Taco Queen never changed. It was smack dab in downtown Shady Lake and was decorated in country western style. There was even a little saddle in the front of the restaurant for kids to sit on while they waited in line to order their food.

Our table was in the corner where two windows met in the front. Back in high school, we liked to see and be seen during lunch. Mostly, I liked to see and Max liked to be seen. But he was a much more popular student than I was and more than a handful of times I wondered why he wanted to date a weirdo like me.

As I walked up, Max wiped his face with a napkin and then jumped up to help pull out the chair for me. The formality was another odd holdover from high school, when he always used the same manners at the taco place that he would have used at a fancy steakhouse or prom.

"Sorry I started without you," he said as I noticed that his plate was already half empty. "I only have a limited amount of time for lunch and I'd rather spend most of it talking to you."

I dipped one of the deep fried tortilla chips into the homemade salsa. Delicious, but also dangerous. I probably consumed an entire day's worth of calories just in tortilla chips every time I came here. I made a mental note to not have a donut today.

"That's alright," I said. "I was running a little late today. I had an odd encounter with Susy Martin as I was about to get ready to leave. She's a guest at the B&B."

I took a bite of my chicken taco. While I

chewed, I tried to decide if I should talk to Max about the case or not. I was leaning towards talking to him about it. But I took another giant bite of my taco to chew on just in case he was going to spill the beans.

But Max was too busy shoveling refried beans and rice into his mouth to say much of anything. Once my mouth was clear of delicious taco, I dropped the information I had gleaned.

"So this Susy told me today that she is actually Earl's cousin," I said nonchalantly as I watched for his reaction. "And now that he is dead, she gets the business and the land."

Max stopped chewing for a moment. I got the distinct feeling that this was all news to him. But he recovered quickly and finished chewing the gigantic bite of enchilada in his mouth before he responded.

"Oh, that is strange," he said. "But I didn't come here to talk about Earl's murder. Which you shouldn't be concerning yourself with anyways."

He gave me a pointed look, but I took a bite of taco and stared out the window while I chewed it, pretending I didn't notice. There weren't that many people out and about today. It was a chilly day, so most people that were out were hurrying to their destination, not lollygagging around. Every once in a while, a large gust of wind would swoop down the street, bringing leaves with it and pushing pedestrians along. Main Street had fun orange and black wreaths with flags advertising the Halloween Hayride on the lampposts that were being blown all over the place today, but managed to keep themselves secured to the post.

We both ate in silence for a few moments. Whereas with Clark I always had to find a way to fill the gaps of silence, Max and I had known each other for so long that silence wasn't awkward. While being with Clark was exciting and new, being with Max was predictable and comfortable.

My phone vibrated in my pocket and I took it out to see I had a text from Mandy.

Get here now! Ralph just sat down with a donut and a cup of coffee.

Suddenly, I realized Max had started talking to me as I had been checking my phone. I needed to get to the Donut Hut fast, but he looked like he was saying something important.

"I'm sorry, I didn't hear what you said. I was reading a text message from Mandy."

"I said we need to figure out our Halloween costume soon so we can start getting them put together," Max said. "We don't really have that much time."

Shoot, I had kind of forgotten about my costume debacle. I couldn't possibly figure it out now. I needed to get to the Donut Hut and figure out a way to get some information out of Ralph.

"You're right," I said. "You know what? I will think about it tonight and get some ideas and maybe we could go out again this week and go over my list. Does that sound good? You need to get back to work anyways, right?"

Max's brow furrowed. He could always tell when I wasn't telling the whole truth. It was the other downside to dating Max again. It wasn't that I wanted to lie to anyone, but like I told Clark, I just managed to get myself into these odd situations.

"Okay," he said slowly. He stood up and opened his arms for a hug.

I let my mind slow down enough to step into his big, muscular arms. As he gave me a gentle squeeze, I let myself forget for just one minute that I needed to not only pick a costume and costume partner, but also to catch a murderer while I made sure the

Halloween Hayride went off without another hitch. It's amazing how much busier I became when I moved back home.

•Chapter 11•

As soon as I waved Max's police cruiser out of sight, I booked it down Main Street, turning at the corner where it intersected with Bridge Street. Once the Donut Hut was in view, I slowed to a walk. I'm sure I was already getting some stares, but I just pretended that I was running because I was really cold. The last thing I needed was for a suspected murderer to see me out of breath from running to talk to him.

I nonchalantly strolled in, letting the bell announce my presence. I casually looked around the cafe as I walked to the counter. Ralph was sitting in the back corner by the bathroom, looking like he was trying to hide. Mandy was waiting for me when I got to the counter.

"Quick, get me a cup of coffee and a donut," I said in a low voice. I had the bare bones of a plan, but mostly I was just going to wing it.

Mandy shoved a coffee cup and a plate with a maple long john donut across the counter at me. My skinny jeans were going to hate me after this. I threw a few dollars on the counter and made my way towards

Ralph.

"Hey there," I said casually as I sat at the tiny table next to his. "I heard about your friend. I'm really sorry for your loss."

Ralph turned and scowled at me. He looked like he thought about saying something, but then shook his head and took another drink of coffee instead. His large hands wrapped all the way around the coffee cup, making it look like he was drinking out of a miniature cup.

"What a bummer it must have been to lose your friend like that," I said, inwardly cringing at my choice of words. "What was he doing out there anyways?"

"It was his land," Ralph said flatly. "He had a right to be there."

"Sure sure," I said nodding. "But he made it very clear that he didn't like the Halloween Hayride, so it wasn't like he was there to help."

Ralph gave a stiff nod. I shoved a large bite of donut in my mouth so I would stop talking for a little bit. I've learned from crime shows that sometimes if you stop talking, the other person will fill the silence. Either way, it was an excuse to eat the donut I had just paid for.

"I remember you from the Hayride

meeting before Earl died," he finally said. "What is your name again?"

"I'm Tessa," I said, extending my hand. Ralph scowled at it before grasping it with his giant hand and giving it a brisk shake. His hand was so large that it wrapped all the way around my hand and I had what I considered to be large hands for a woman. "I am the marketing chair on the Halloween Hayride committee. I'm just hoping to get all of this stuff wrapped up so that the Hayride can go off without a hitch."

"I hope it all gets wrapped up too," Ralph snorted. "I've been told I can't leave town until the police tell me I can."

"Oh that's terrible," I said as I innocently stirred my coffee. "Here you've lost your friend and now you are stuck in this little town. They should really be more understanding."

Ralph sat back in his chair and crossed his arms across his chest. He seemed to be sizing me up, so I did my best to puff myself up, but also look like a concerned citizen which, I guess I actually was in this situation. He leaned towards me and motioned for me to move closer. I scooted myself as close as I could comfortably be to him.

"It is a terrible situation, but I'll let you in on a little secret," he said. "I was actually with Earl that night out at the field."

Even though I kind of knew that, my eyes grew wide and my mouth popped open, but I managed to not say something stupid for once. I simply nodded my head, willing him to keep talking.

"Earl wanted to go out and pull a few pranks," Ralph said quietly. "You know, sugar in the gas tank of the tractor, nailing some shed doors shut, that kind of thing. I didn't really think it was a good idea, but I went along with him. I mean, that is what I was paid to do after all."

I nodded, wondering if this conversation was going to lead to a confession. Was I sitting next to a murderer? I sneaked a look at his feet. He was wearing large, outdoorsy boots that would probably match the footprints I found at the scene. I gulped and looked back at his face.

"While we were out there, I finally got fed up with him," Ralph said. He took a sip of coffee and sat back, thinking for a moment. I shoved another bite of maple donut in my mouth to make sure something stupid didn't fall out of my mouth again. "I asked him why exactly the Hayride was such a big deal. Obviously it was a fight he wasn't going to win. So at that point, I said he was just being bitter."

"And what did he think about that?" I asked before taking another bite of donut. I couldn't blow this entire thing just because I couldn't keep my mouth shut. But my full stomach was also telling me to maybe slow down a little bit on the eating for a while.

"He did not like it," Ralph said. "Earl fired me on the spot. I shoved him a little and then ran to the car and took off. I figured I'd get the last laugh because he'd probably end up calling me for a ride. But drove back home and ended up falling asleep on the couch. I woke up the next morning to the news he was dead. So I'm not really sure what happened. But I do know I wasn't a part of it."

"Wow, that is quite the story," I said. "That must be really heartbreaking to have your friend murdered right after being with him."

"It is sad, but please stop calling him my friend," Ralph said. "We weren't friends. He employed me as an assistant and bodyguard. I didn't even really like the man. But his stature and ability to make enemies as soon as he met them meant he paid me well."

"Oh, I just assumed that you were friends because you spent all of your time with him," I said. From what I heard, they were literally always together. Why else besides being friends would they spend all of that time together?

"Yeah, well I had my reasons," Ralph said. He tipped his coffee mug up until he drained it. "But believe me when I say that I didn't like the man at all."

"Well I'm still sorry for your loss," I said.

"Thanks," Ralph said. He pushed back his chair and stood up. "I should be going now."

He walked out of the Donut Hut, his shoulders slumped forward. Even hunched over, he still towered over everyone and had to duck as he walked out the front door. I sat back and popped the last bite of donut in my mouth. This conversation had been enlightening, but I was still at an impasse. Ralph wouldn't want to kill Earl because Earl signed his paycheck. Even if he didn't like the guy, would he kill him and lose his job?

I drank the dregs of my coffee and stood up, brushing donut crumbs off of me. My Mexican lunch, donut, and coffee all caught up with me and I was feeling so full that I felt sick. I glanced at the clock over the cash register and realized my parents probably wanted me back almost an hour ago.

I walked towards the door of the Donut Hut, casting a look at Mandy that told her I would text her later. I flipped my phone open to see that my mother had tried to call me three times. I listened to the voicemail that she left. It wasn't anything urgent,but she made it seem urgent. Apparently the B&B was out of milk and that prompted the emergency call. I made a note to swing by the gas station to grab a gallon of milk. My mom preferred me to stop there because milk was ten cents cheaper and she always loved finding a bargain.

I walked back to the station wagon while I thought back about the conversation I had just had with Ralph. I had this gut feeling that he wasn't the right suspect. But the police thought he was and he definitely had a motive. Plus in this case, the boot print fit.

•Chapter 12•

After returning home triumphantly bearing many gallons of milk for the guests of the bed and breakfast and my family, I was assigned desk duty for a couple of hours. Now, at the motel that my parents also own, desk duty is busy. I have to answer the phone, make reservations, help guests who come by. The motel has fifty rooms and often, many are filled as Shady Lake sits just off of the intersection of two major freeways. The motel gets many travelers and truck drivers who just see the sign from the freeway and decide to take a chance to find a room.

But at the B&B, desk duty is usually quite boring. First of all, there aren't that many guests because we only have five guest rooms. And most of the guests have plans during the day, whether they are out and about in town or relaxing around the B&B. So desk duty ends up being a lot of sitting around and answering the phone every once in a while.

That was just what I needed though because I wanted to make a list of suspects. So far I had a few people who were definitely suspects and a few who might be. I got out a piece of paper and started my list with the two biggest suspects, at least when it came to looking at the clues.

Ralph-big boot print that might match his boot, admits he was at the field and pushed Earl that night

Ronald-found his watch at the site of the murder, wants to protect the Halloween Hayride and the money Shady Lake gets from it.

I sat back for a moment and thought about the facts. Who else would want Earl out of the picture? I had only seen him twice around town, but then I remembered the second time. He and Candy were on the street corner having some sort of argument the morning before he died. They both didn't look very happy. And that was less than a day before he was killed. I added Candy to the list.

Candy-argued with Earl that day

The last person I added was Susy. I still didn't know much about her, but she had practically handed me a motive. Plus her dirty car meant she had been somewhere out in the country recently.

Susy-mad about inheritance, car was dusty

I had to admit that the last piece of "evidence" was pretty weak, but if I dig, maybe I could find something else going on there. Not that I wanted to talk too much to that sour puss.

Overall, I felt like I was spinning in circles. I wondered if the police felt the same way. Sure Ralph seemed to have evidence piling up against him but, for obvious reasons, the police didn't know about Ronald's watch that I had found at the scene of the crime.

"Ahem."

I looked up to see Susy clearing her throat in front of me. I jumped a little and scrambled to cover up the piece of paper that I had stupidly labeled SUSPECTS in large letters. Papers flew all over the desk and the floor in my hurry. I winced a little at how oblivious I had been.

"Hello Ms. Martin," I said in my syrupy retail voice once I had gathered myself a bit. "How can I help you?"

"I'm actually feeling quite ill and I was wondering if I could maybe get a ginger ale in my room?"

She did look rather green. The poor woman must be taking her cousin's death pretty hard.

"Of course," I said. "You go on up and I will bring one in just a moment."

I practically skipped to the kitchen once she was out of sight. This was just the moment I needed to try and get some more information about her. I pushed open the swinging door to the kitchen to see my father sitting at the table. We had a dining room with a large table for the guests and for our family dinners. But the kitchen was much more intimate, with a small square table over by the kitchen windows. Only four of us still lived here: my parents, me, and my youngest brother Tank. We didn't need a full dinner table every night any more.

"Hi Pumpkin," my dad said. "What are you so happy about?"

"Oh nothing," I said. "Just getting down to solving a mystery I've been curious about."

I grimaced a little bit as I realized what I had said, but I hoped he hadn't caught it. I opened the fridge and pulled out a ginger ale. We weren't big pop drinkers, but we tried to keep some of the most requested kinds for the guests to enjoy.

"You aren't trying to investigate that murder, are you?" my father asked. He had the local paper open on the table in front of him, but instead of looking at the high school sports scores, he was raising an eyebrow at me.

For a moment, I wondered if I should try to play it off like it was nothing, but my dad had always been able to read me like a book. I think it has something to do with the fact that I'm the kid that is most like him, personality-wise at least.

"Maybe a little bit," I squirmed and looked at my feet, not able to look him in the eye. "I'm not getting in the way, but since I found the body, I kind of feel a responsibility to figure out what happened to Earl."

My dad sighed a long sigh and shut the paper. I could see the front page had a big picture of the orange tractor sitting in the middle of the field and the headline shouted "HALLOWEEN HAYRIDE IS STILL ON." I was pretty sure the byline was Chelsea. I'm also sure she was hoping to have more of a lead to report on but from what I gathered, the police were playing this pretty close to the vest. I'm sure she was not happy about having to make her front page story about the Halloween Hayride instead of the more exciting murder.

"Honey, you should not get wrapped up

in this," he said. "I look the other way when you meddle in friendships and gossip. I even look the other way when you get yourself entwined in the problems of the guests who stay here. But I can't let you meddle with a murder."

"Oh Dad," I said, rolling my eyes at him. I know he was concerned, but I am a grown woman. I don't need my dad to take care of me. "I'm fine. It's not like I would do something dumb."

"Well, I think investigating a murder on your own is kind of dumb," he said. "But to each their own, I guess."

He opened the newspaper in front of him, shaking it to get the folds and wrinkles out. I wasn't about to let him get the last word this time.

"The apple doesn't fall far from the tree," I said with as straight of a face as I could pull. But as soon as my dad snorted out a laugh, I busted out laughing. I prided myself on being the only one of my siblings who could never fail to make him laugh.

My dad just waved a hand at me as if to say "get out of here." Then he turned a page of the paper and immersed himself back into the world of local news. I grabbed a tray and beside the can of ginger ale, I put a glass and a bowl of ice cubes with a little set of tongs. It was much fancier than I normally would do, but I tried to go all out to impress this suburban woman.

As I pushed myself out the swinging kitchen door, I had a flash of a memory with Peter as I saw the dining room table. Peter grew up in a small family that was just his parents, his brother, and himself. The first time I invited him to dinner with my family, he was gobsmacked. All five of us kids and my parents sat down with Peter. The table had been loaded down as it was a Sunday dinner. Roast chicken, mashed potatoes, salad, all sorts of delicious food lined the table.

We all bowed our heads and said grace before starting to load up our plates. I had realized that Peter was so out of his element that he was just sitting in his chair staring at everyone instead of filling his plate with food. I started slopping food onto his plate along with my own plate in a crazed way. When he finally noticed what I was doing, he asked me what was going on.

"If you don't get it now, you aren't gonna eat," I had apparently shouted in his face.

It had taken me a while to figure out why he was so out of place among the food slopping and my brother tossing a roll to everyone at the table. Then I went to dinner at Peter's house. Everyone sat down very quietly and passed the serving dishes around the table. Everyone used manners and only made polite conversation instead of burping the alphabet and singing their new favorite song between bites.

Later on, I had asked Peter why in the world he stayed with me after that first family dinner where he was obviously uncomfortable.

"You push me out of my comfort zone," Peter had said. "I like that."

I left that memory in the dining room. I paused at the foot of the stairs, wondering if I should try to plan out what I wanted to say a little more. But so far, winging it was working for me. So I started up the stairs, hoping a ginger ale would help me solve a murder.

•Chapter 13•

At the top of the wide, sweeping stairs, I stopped to catch my breath. I had been eating too many donuts and not getting enough exercise lately. I made a mental note to myself to try and change that, even though I knew that wouldn't happen at least until the holiday season was over. I suppose I'd have to make a New Years resolution to help.

I walked to the end of the hall and knocked on the door of the Cardinal Room. Each of the rooms in the inn was named after a bird that is common to Minnesota and that the guests may even see in our vast yard. Besides the Cardinal Room, there was also the Blue Jay Room, the Chickadee Room, the Woodpecker Room, and the Hummingbird Suite, which was also our honeymoon suite.

My dad has always enjoyed bird watching. He wasn't one of those crazy bird watchers with a gigantic list of bird species they want to see and check off. Instead, he enjoys sitting in the bay window and watching birds. There are a few bird identification books and a pair of binoculars

in a drawer next to my dad's favorite chair.
When my parents decided to open the bed
and breakfast, my dad jumped at the chance
to use birds as the theme.

"Come in," Susy's weak voice replied
from within.

I pushed open the door and brought the
tray inside. Susy was lying on the bed all
wrapped up in the quilt, looking like death
warmed over. My dad had been adamant
about not putting televisions in the guest
rooms even though we tried to tell him that
was a terrible idea. Susy had found a way
around it and was watching some sort of
house hunting show on a laptop that was
sitting next to her on the bed.

"Here you go Ms. Martin," I said. "I
found a ginger ale for you. Are you feeling
alright?"

"Oh yes, it is just a little tummy bug," she
said. She started to push herself up on her
elbows, but shut her eyes and lowered
herself back down again.

"I can pour it in the glass if you'd like," I
offered. She waved her hand ever so
slightly, so I took that to mean I should go
ahead. As I poured, I figured I'd take some
time to ask some more questions.

"So, I know you said you didn't see eye to

eye with your cousin, but were you ever close?" I asked. If they had once been close, that could explain why she was so upset.

"No, never," Susy said. "But I was close to my uncle. That is why it was quite a surprise when I found out the business went to Earl. Uncle Gordon and I used to talk on the phone everyday. I knew that he didn't think women should run a car business, but I didn't think he would give it to my incompetent cousin instead of me. I suppose he didn't think Earl would be so terrible at managing the business."

I set the glass of ginger ale on the nightstand next to Susy's head. It was good to hear that Gordon hadn't been as lonely as he had seemed. Susy gave another attempt to sit up. This time, she was able to hoist herself up to a sitting position, even if she was still a bit slumped over.

The quilt slipped down and I saw that she was wearing a light blue silk pajama top. I was amazed at how despite her illness, she managed to still look somewhat put together. I thought about the giant t-shirt and pajama pants I slept in. I had won the shirt in a raffle at the county fair and the pants used to be Peter's. I wasn't ready to give up the pants, but I added "new pajama shirt" to my mental to-do list.

"I bet that made you pretty upset," I said. "I know it would make me angry if my good for nothing cousin was running a family business into the ground. Did your uncle leave you anything?"

"Yes, so I really shouldn't complain," she said. "He left me everything else. I'm already in the process of selling his house, but I kept the car. That's the one I've been driving. He also left me all of his money, which was quite a lot. Uncle Gordon was no dummy when it came to the stock market."

Susy took a sip of ginger ale. Apparently that helped, because she immediately took three more small sips after it. So her financial motive wasn't really a motive. I guess she still may have killed Earl because she was mad about the car lot. But it wasn't like she needed the money. It sounded like Gordon had made sure she was financially secure even if he didn't trust her to run some rinky dink, small town used car dealership.

"Well that's good," I said. "I think you got the better end of the deal, honestly. You seem like someone comfortable in the suburbs. It isn't like you'd want to stay here in Shady Lake."

"Lately I haven't been so sure about the burbs," she said. "There are a couple of reasons that I'm looking to slow down my life and really enjoy it. Shady Lake seems great for that. I've been going back and forth about whether I should sell Uncle Gordon's house or live in it."

"It really is great for that," I said. My life had certainly needed some slowing down after Peter died and Shady Lake had provided.

"I should be getting back to the desk," I said. I didn't want to overstay my welcome, so I grabbed the tray and headed towards the door. "Let me know if you need anything else."

"Will do," Susy said. "Thanks again. I really needed this."

I smiled at her and let myself out of her room. I smiled to myself as I walked back down to the kitchen. One nice thing about a small town was these little glimpses of humanity. Somehow, these sorts of breaking down of barriers just didn't happen when I lived in the big city.

When I got back to the kitchen to put the tray away, my dad was gone. The newspaper was folded up nicely on the table. After I shoved the tray back into a cabinet, I walked over to take a closer look at the front page.

There was something about the picture of the tractor that just didn't seem right, but I couldn't put my finger on it. I scanned it closely, looking for details that were out of place. I even squinted a little, but no matter what it just looked like a giant orange tractor sitting in the middle of the field.

I wondered if I should try to go out to the field again to get a closer look. But I knew that wasn't feasible for two reasons. There was no way I could convince Mandy to go with me again. Plus I'd want to go during the daytime, but that was not a good idea. I really didn't want to get caught out there snooping around.

When I got back to the front desk, I sat down and checked the phone messages. Like usual, there were none. Most of our business occurred online, so phone calls were rare. As I surfed the web a little on the out dated desktop my parents kept for business use, my phone buzzed.

I flipped it open and instead of a message from Mandy, I was looking at a message from Ronald.

Can you come to my office to meet about the Hayride? I have a few things I'd like to touch base on.

I looked at the clock. It was almost 2, which was when the part time evening worker Helen came in. Helen had worked at the motel's front desk for years and when my parents opened the B&B, they gave her the chance to move over here. She was a quiet, gray haired woman who loved to make small talk with the guests. Once she arrived, I'd be free as a bird.

I'll be over as soon as Helen arrives at 2. See you then.

I set my phone down and went back to putzing around when my phone buzzed again. Instead of Ronald, this time it was a message from Clark.

Hey Tess, I have a few ideas for our costumes. Let's go out soon to discuss. Don't worry, they are better than ketchup and mustard ;)

Uh oh. I had been so deep in my investigation that I had forgotten about my costume debacle again. I still hadn't really decided what to do about that. I had told Clark first that I would dress up with him. But I know Max would be depending on me more and would be more heartbroken if I said I couldn't.

I didn't text Clark back right away because I needed some more time to think.

And another nice thing about a flip phone?
No read receipts.

•Chapter 14•

Moving back to my hometown after some time away was odd partly because I felt like everything should be exactly the same when I had left, but obviously things had changed in the decade that I had been gone. So while the buildings were still the same, sometimes the business inside was different from before. One new thing was the new courthouse in town. It wasn't totally new, but it had been totally redone. The new courthouse housed all of the city and county offices along with the DMV and a small jail. I had driven by it a few times, but never been inside until today.

I walked in the main doors into a beautiful vestibule. When they rebuilt the courthouse, they had maintained the beautiful old building, but simply revamped it and added onto it. The main vestibule was a large, open space with a large dome and a large mural surrounded by beautiful woodworking. I imagined it looked the same as it did when my great grandfather moved here.

The rotunda had a large spiral staircase that ran around the edge of the round vestibule and up to the second floor. I climbed the stairs, admiring the beautifully redone wood and the wonderful stained glass window halfway up that threw colored flecks of lights around the room.

At the top of the stairs, there was a set of double doors that led to all of the offices of city officials. I pushed it open and was shocked to see Candy sitting at one of the desks inside. There was a nameplate on her desk that listed her title as "Assistant to the Mayor." She certainly did well for herself, so why was she cozying up to Earl? And I have to admit, I was a little surprised to find her at work after her boyfriend had just been murdered a few days ago. But they say that people grieve in all sorts of ways so I tried not to judge her.

I walked up to her desk and waited while she ended a phone call. After I got closer, I noticed that she wasn't quite as put together as she had seemed. There were a few platinum curls that weren't quite in the right place and her mascara had been hastily applied so there were some black marks around her eyes. Her fingernails were painted, but it had grown out a little. Her desk had crumpled up tissues strewn all over what seemed like a usually tidy area. It looked like she was trying hard to look put together, but just wasn't able to live up to her usual standard.

"Tessa?" she said. Her voice was still just as high pitched as it had been in high school. Candy had always tried a little too hard to fit in. She had been really nice, but always a little odd.

"Hey Candy," I said, putting a comforting hand on her shoulder for a moment. "How are you holding up? I'm so sorry for your loss."

"Thank you Tessy," she said. I cringed at the elementary school nickname I had long since shed. She dabbed at her eye with one of the wadded up tissues she grabbed off of her desk. "It is so hard, but I know that we will get justice for my Earl."

"Yes we will," I said. I reached out and grabbed a hold of her hand to give it a squeeze. I tried not to think about the tears and boogers that were probably on her hands judging from the amount of tissues scattered around. "I'm sorry to say I didn't know much about Earl."

Candy sniffled a few times. She reached out and turned a gold frame to face me. Inside was a picture of Candy and Earl that appeared to have been taken at the bowling alley. Earl looked like he'd had a few too many and he was wearing torn jeans and a stained t-shirt. He was focused on something off camera. Candy was draped over him wearing a pair of denim shorts that were just a bit too short and button up plaid shirt that was just a bit too tight.

She looked a bit off the mark, as usual. But mostly she looked like she should be standing next to someone else. Someone who seemed to appreciate her a bit more. If this was the best picture Candy could find of her and Earl to frame for work, that was saying something about their relationship.

"Earl was trying so hard to run the dealership," Candy said. I tried my best to keep my eyeballs firmly in place instead of rolling because from everything I'd heard, he was not trying so hard. "He was such a go-getter. And he just wanted to do things differently, but when he tried to change things, everyone got all upset. I just wish they could have seen what he was trying to do."

I was pretty sure that what he was trying to do was to line his own pockets with cash, but I managed to hold my tongue. I glanced around and spotted an empty chair that I hauled over to sit next to Candy. I settled myself into the uncomfortable, vinyl covered chair and set my purse on the floor next to me.

"Tell me some more," I prompted her as I leaned towards her. "I'd love to hear how you met."

Partly, I just wanted to hear more to add to my investigation. But I also felt sorry for Candy. She had always wanted a boyfriend in high school. She managed to go out on a few dates, but she always came on way too strong. Candy had once told us that she longed for that fairy tale type of love at first sight where they quickly go on to marry and live happily ever after. So far, that hadn't happened for her.

"When Earl came to town, I was thrilled," Candy said. "I tried for almost two weeks to track him down because I saw his picture and thought he was just so handsome. I also heard he had inherited the car dealership and I was interested to hear if he was going to stick around town."

Poor Candy was much more transparent than she thought. She had grown up living in a trailer park and had once confided in us that she didn't want to end up a part of the working poor like her parents. I'm sure the thought of a new, potentially rich man in town had been very exciting for her.

"I finally tracked him down at the bowling alley," she said with a smile on her face. "That is where we took this picture. It was the first time we had met. I told him I'd been looking all over town for him and he said that he'd heard a pretty blond had been looking for him and that must be me. That was all I needed. I was smitten."

That made me ache a little inside. Poor Candy had always wanted to fall in love and Earl had been there for her. And then he had died, leaving Candy alone once again. No matter how slimy Earl was, I got the feeling that he had actually loved Candy.

"What a lovely story," I said, plastering a smile on my face. Candy just stared at the photo with the smile fading slightly.

"I'm just so sad our story is over before it even really started," Candy said. "We had been talking about marriage and instead, this happened. It doesn't help that we parted on bad terms. We had an argument that morning."

"Oh really?" I said. I remembered driving by them that morning, wondering what was going on. But Candy's back had been to me. Only Earl had seen my roll by.

"Yes and it is a horrible thing to think about," she said. "I confronted him because I thought he may be cheating on me. I couldn't believe he would do that to me, but he assured me that he wasn't cheating."

"Well at least you knew that he didn't cheat," I said.

"We still didn't leave on a good note," Candy said. "I was still pretty upset because he had canceled a date with me and I heard he was out for coffee with another woman. I told him I believed him, but that I was still mad and I couldn't be around him."

Her face crumpled and tears started falling down her face. I fetched a few more tissues for her from a box on a nearby shelf. She gratefully used them to dry her tears.

"Are you okay Candy?" I asked after a few moments. I had to meet with Ronald, but I didn't want to leave her in such a flustered state.

"I'm okay," she said. She glanced at her wrist where she must have worn a watch usually. But her wrist was empty today. She must have forgotten it in her flustered state. "You're here for a meeting with Ronald, right?"

"Yup, he wanted to see me about the Halloween Hayride."

"Well I'm sorry I kept you," Candy said as she wiped her eyes again. "Go on in. He's been waiting for you."

I took one last look at her tear streaked face and I reached over to squeeze her hand one more time.

"It will all be okay Candy," I said. She nodded at me. "Here, let me write down my number for you in case you need to talk some more."

After jotting down my number on a scrap of paper, I turned to the door that had Ronald's name on it. I'm not sure how I got so lucky, but I was somehow talking to all of the suspects today. Too bad I wasn't getting anywhere so far.

•Chapter 15•

Ronald's office looked more like the office of a high school principal than a mayor. It was a bit messy, with a book shelf that looked like the books he took out were subsequently thrown back around the ones still standing up. His desk was currently covered in Halloween knick-knacks and he even had a banner of smiling jack-o-lanterns hanging above the large windows that looked out over Shady Lake. Somehow the oddness of it seemed just like Ronald in a nutshell.

"Ah, Tessa! Just the woman I wanted to see."

"Hello Ronald," I said. He was sitting in a big leather chair behind his desk, looking genuinely excited to see me. He motioned for me to sit down in one of the chairs across from him.

"I wanted to touch base with you about the Halloween Hayride," he said. Ronald folded his large hands on top of a stack of papers in front of him. " I know we are getting closer to it, but the investigation is still pretty up in the air, although from what I hear, they may be bringing in a suspect soon."

"Oh really?" I asked. I realized I was playing innocent to get more information, which is the exact same thing Mandy does that drives me nuts. I was starting to see why she did it because it was pretty effective to get more info, at least with people who don't know you super well. "If you don't mind me asking, who are they bringing in?"

"Well, I'm not totally for sure," Ronald said, fidgeting with a little witch shaped toy on his desk. "I was kind of hoping that you would know."

"Oh, well I have actually heard a few rumors, but nothing solid," I said.

Technically Ronald was on my list of suspects so I wasn't sure if I should tell him anything or not. Was he guilty and wanted to hear if he was going to be arrested soon? Or was he innocent and just totally in the dark? Currently, he was playing with a small fidget toy that was shaped like a pumpkin. Could he really be the murderer?

"By the way, did you ever find your watch?" I asked. "I remember you had lost it the other day."

"Oh, that," Ronald said, his face contorting into a grimace for a split second before he caught himself. "I'm not quite sure. I kind of forgot to look for it."

For a few moments, our conversation hung in the air between us. I looked around for something to cut the awkwardness, but I didn't think I should play with the toys on his desk and I was a little disappointed to see that his candy dish was only filled with candy corn, something that despite my love of all things seasonal, I did not even consider to be candy.

"Why don't we just discuss the Halloween Hayride?" I suggested after a few moments. "I really should have stopped and gotten us a few coffees and some donuts from Mandy. I'll have to remember that next time."

"Oh, no donuts," Ronald chuckled as he patted his stomach. "I'm supposed to be on a bit of a diet. Mellie thinks I've gained too much weight and she is worried about me gaining even more during this holiday season. So she told me that if I stuck to my diet until Thanksgiving, the rest of the holiday season would be less of a worry when it came to my weight."

There were many things that Melinda hated, such as anything seasonal, joyful, or traditional. But one of her biggest pet peeves was Ronald's weight. As far as I could remember, Ronald has always been a bit overweight. He appears to be the sort of person who is also healthy while carrying around a few pounds.

"Oh, I'm sorry," I said. The mere mention of Melinda seemed to suck all of the happiness out of the air. I always wondered what their home life was like. I imagined a battle of good and evil was constantly being waged in their living room.

"But that's alright," Ronald said conspiratorially as he pointed at the pumpkin shaped candy dish that looked like it belonged in my grandmother's kitchen. "Mellie doesn't know about this candy corn. You can help yourself if you'd like."

"No thank you," I said. I tried to think up an excuse, but I couldn't, so I decided to just switch topics. "Now, the Halloween Hayride. Have the police released the tractor from evidence yet?"

"Not yet, but they said they would by the end of this week," Ronald said. "If they don't, I have had several citizens offer their tractors for a night or two, so no worries."

"What about the haunted house?" I asked. "Has Clark updated you on how the plans for that are going?"

"No, I was going to assign that duty to you," Ronald said with a wink. "I know you and Clark are pretty close friends."

I smiled politely. Shoot, now I would have to discuss Halloween costumes with him. I made a mental note to text him back after the meeting and suggest we get together in the next couple of days. I also made a mental note to actually figure out which man to turn down and then come up with a list of possible costumes.

The rest of my meeting with Ronald was mostly uneventful except for things related to the Halloween Hayride. We talked about the list of volunteers, the tractor driving safety event we were hosting the next weekend for everyone who would be driving the Hayride, and the menu of food that would be available for sale. It was all pretty boring, especially considering the the Hayride stayed pretty much the same year after year. The only thing that typically changed was the order in which we set up the scary scenes the tractor drove through.

I was just about to stand up to leave when Ronald looked around nervously. He was wringing his hands and a worried expression settled onto his face.

"Umm, Tessa? Can I confide something in you?"

"Sure Ronald," I said. I was used to people confiding things in me. I was someone who apparently had a nice and trusting face. I was often roped into long conversations with strangers or near strangers while out and about where my Minnesota nice upbringing battled against my can't stop talking mouth. "What's wrong?"

"I was actually out at the hayride field on the day when Earl was murdered," Ronald said. He was almost twitching, he was so nervous. "I had gone out earlier that day to practice driving the tractor. I'm not very good at it and I really didn't want to embarrass myself or the entire town by being totally incompetent."

Whoa. For a moment I felt like time had slowed down a bit. Even after finding the watch out at the field, I still figured that Ronald couldn't possibly be the murderer. But he was admitting to being out at the field. Why would he tell me that? Did he know I had the watch? The wheels in my head were spinning with possibilities.

"I just thought you should know," he said. "The police have asked me a few questions and I don't think I'm their main suspect, but they are keeping me in the dark so I'm a little worried. I swear I didn't kill him. Sure, I didn't like the nincompoop, but I never would have harmed him."

I wanted to believe him, but the watch I had found told me otherwise. I decided I really needed to make my exit from his office. I might be in over my head a little here. For a moment, I thought my dad might be right.

"I will keep that in mind, Ronald. And like I said, I won't let anything happen to the Halloween Hayride. I promise it will go off without a hitch. Well, without anymore hitches I guess."

After a long, Minnesota goodbye discussion about what my parents and each of my siblings have been up to lately, I finally left Ronald's office. Candy was on the phone, thankfully, otherwise I would have been roped into another long goodbye. Instead, I was able to give a small wave of my hand and make my leave. She waved her long fingernails at me, looking more like her normal self. Her face was no longer tear streaked and her desk had significantly less tissues than it had before.

As I walked down the beautiful, winding

staircase, I considered the facts of the case so far. Every time I thought I was ruling someone out, I was actually ruling them in. The crime shows made it look so easy. The detective always seemed to know exactly what was going on and who did it. It was like once they saw the initial facts of the case, they automatically knew who did it and then just slowly investigated until they could definitively prove they were right. Well, at least I knew no one would ever make my life into a television show.

•Chapter 16•

Once I was back at the house, I made my way to my bedroom. My bedroom is in the part of the B&B that guests are not allowed to go in. It is for just my parents, siblings, and I to enjoy. It consists of part of the second floor along with an addition that was built on the back of the house and on top of our garage. It sounds kind of like a jumbled up monster house when I describe it like that, but it really is quite charming.

The private section of the B&B was the perfect size before I moved in, but I had to take over the small library in the private section of the house. My youngest brother Tank actually has a nice suite over the garage, but I told my parents they didn't have to kick him out of it. Besides, he would graduate soon enough and then, if I was still living here, I could move in there.

I don't plan on living at the B&B forever. I'd love to buy my own little house in town. The only problem with living in a small town is that all of the houses for sale tend to be old and need work. There is nothing wrong with a fixer upper, but I just wasn't used to that right now. Living in the city, the worst thing I'd have to do when we moved was change the paint colors. Remodeling and redoing a kitchen or bathroom just seemed totally overwhelming.

I flopped down on my bed and decided I needed to message Clark immediately before I forgot again. I would have to get together with him soon and I think he was the one I would have to let down. He would have no problem finding someone else to dress up with if he wanted to. He had ladies falling all over him most of the time. Max didn't have the same luxury of being the new, handsome man in town. I typed out a quick message for him.

Are you free tonight? Ronald gave me the task of checking up on you and the haunted house. ;)

I set my phone down on my nightstand and shut my eyes for a few moments. I started to run through everything that I had learned in the last couple of days. I had always been a listmaker, but this time I decided to keep my list in my head instead of written down like the last one that Susy almost saw.

Ralph didn't actually like Earl and he definitely wore boots that probably matched the print I found. He was also the last person to see Earl alive as far as I knew.

Susy was mad about Earl getting the car dealership and land and her car was dusty and dirty.

Ronald had lost his watch and I had found it out in the field. He also admitted to being at the field that day.

Candy had argued with Earl that day and said that she was still mad because he may be seeing another woman.

As I mulled over the suspects and clues, my phone buzzed on the nightstand. I flipped it open expecting to have a message from Clark, but I was surprised to see it was from Max instead.

Hey Sweet Thing, I'd like to take you out again soon. Are you free if I stop over with some coffee?

Clark hadn't gotten back to me yet, so I figured it would be as good time as ever for me to try and pick Max's brain a little bit about the murder and to talk about our Halloween costumes.

Sure, you can stop by. I'll be waiting for you in the front room.

I took a look in the mirror. I wasn't one for fashion, but I did try to look good most of the time. Small town living meant that if you didn't look good, everyone would know you ran to the store in your pajamas and bedhead. I was wearing my normal fall uniform of a pair of jeans and a plaid shirt. My hair was in a long, messy braid that was pulled over one shoulder. And I didn't really wear much makeup, but when I get up in the mornings I always put on eye liner. So I guess I look as good as I usually do.

I put my phone in my pocket and traipsed down the stairs and through the door that separated our private area with the B&B area. Susy was in the sitting room. She had a book in one hand and a package of crackers beside her. I gave her a small wave and she smiled back at me as she waved a half-eaten cracker at me.

My bottom had just barely hit the seat when the front door opened and Max appeared holding two travel cups of coffee. He must have just figured I would say yes because there was no way he could get coffee and get here that fast.

He gave me a cheeky smile as he handed me my coffee which I took to mean he knew what I was thinking. I sat down in one of the wing chairs in the window and Max sat in the other. He was in his uniform, so he must be on duty. The nice thing about a small town was that there sometimes wasn't much for him to do so he was able to take breaks like this.

"Thanks for being free to have coffee with me right now," he said with a smile. "I've been having a pretty slow day at work."

"I thought you'd be really busy considering we just had murder," I said, arching an eyebrow. Max smirked at me.

"You'd think, right?" he said. He took a sip of coffee before looking at me slyly. "So, tell the truth. Have you put any thought at all into our Halloween costume?"

I looked out the window, avoiding his gaze and he knew it. I pretended to be very interested in my coffee while he giggled to himself.

"Well, at least one of us has done the legwork needed to make a great costume," he said. He tossed a piece of paper on the table beside me. On it was written a list of ten costume ideas, including quarterback and cheerleader and cop and robber. I smiled at the sight of his familiar chicken scratch. It was probably illegible to most people, but I'd spent years reading it and could figure it out without much trouble.

I read through the list and then looked up, arching an eyebrow at him. The cop and robber idea was particularly unclever even though he had indicated next to it that I would be the cop while he was the robber, which was a little better.

"Okay, I know most of them aren't even original," he said, putting his hands up in the air. "But to be fair, you didn't come up with any ideas. So I win on that front."

"You've got me on that one," I admitted. "Do you have a pen? I'll narrow this down real quick. How about I narrow it down to three choices and we will decide together from that."

"Sounds good," he said. He handed me a pen from his breast pocket and I got to work. I had to admit, he had a few out of the box ideas and a few that were actually pretty good. I crossed off the few that were really dumb right away. That meant cop and robber was the first one to go. Even if we switched roles, it still seemed too cliche to me to have a cop dress up as a cop.

Suddenly, Max's phone rang. He fished it out of his shirt pocket and took a look at the screen. His eyes popped open in surprise. I tried to surreptitiously watch him while he answered it.

"Max here," he said into the phone. "Mhmm. Mhmm. Okay."

I was dying in the chair next to him. This could be related to murder case and he was giving me nothing to go on. I took a sip of coffee and sat back, pretending to be immensely interested in the list of costumes. Max shifted in his chair, trying to turn away from me, but he couldn't manage to turn his large body much in the narrow chairs.

"Do you need me to help bring him in?" Max asked as quietly as he could without actually whispering. "Ralph's a pretty big guy."

I knew it. I knew they would be bringing him in soon. Max noticed my triumphant look and silently slapped his forehead, realizing he had failed at keeping his conversation a secret.

"Well no matter what, I'm on my way," he said. He pressed the end button and looked over at me, rolling his eyes at my glee.

"Just don't go trying to investigate any more," he said. "We were finally able to arrest our suspect so we don't need you to do anything. I mean, we didn't need you to do anything before, but we really don't need you to do anything now."

"Aww, I didn't know you thought so highly of me," I said. "Come on, I'll walk you out."

I walked by Max's chair to lead him to the front door. Max stood up and grabbed my shoulder, spinning me around into a hug. We were almost the same height, so I rested my chin on his shoulder as he squeezed me tight.

"I'm so glad you came back to town," he said. "I didn't know just how much I missed you until you came back."

My eyes welled up with tears.

"I feel the same way about you," I said. I was so glad we had reconnected, even though we weren't quite sure where our relationship might go.

•Chapter 17•

As I walked Max out to his squad car, Clark's truck pulled up next to it. Uh oh, I had a feeling this wasn't going to end well. I felt like I'd swallowed a big rock that was just sitting in my stomach. While Max and Clark actually liked each other quite a lot as friends, when it came to me they were definitely in competition. It was a friendly, but also heated competition that I neither encouraged nor discouraged. It was just a fact of my life.

"Hey there Max," Clark said as he hopped out of his pickup. "I'm surprised to see you here. Tessa texted me earlier to ask if I'd like to go out tonight."

"Well I had a little free time and figured I'd spend it here discussing our Halloween costume," Max said with a smile. "Good timing though. I just got a call that I need to take, so I was just leaving. No need to get into an argument."

"What do you mean discussing your Halloween costume?" Clark said. My heart leapt into my throat. "Tessa and I are dressing up together."

"Sorry partner," Max said. "But Tessa

and I were just deciding on what we wanted to be together."

Clark looked at me with a pained expression on his face. I really didn't think he would take it as hard as he was. But I also figured I would be the one to give him the news, not Max. The disappointment was probably doubled when it came from your romantic rival.

Max hopped in his squad car and gave one last triumphant wave as he pulled out of the driveway. He just couldn't help but rub his win in Clark's face. Clark turned and looked at me. He was still looking really hurt. I figured if anything, his temper would mean he would be angry. But he just looked sad. I wondered briefly if I had chosen the wrong man to dress up with. I quickly shot that down because that line of thinking would bring me nowhere.

"So when were you going to tell me that you didn't want to be in a costume together," Clark asked.

"Tonight," I admitted. I shuffled my feet a little bit as I tried to avoid making eye contact. "You both asked me to dress up as a couple within an hour of each other and I panicked and said yes to both of you. I've been trying to figure out what to do about it ever since. I kind of got myself in over my head with this one."

"Yeah, you did," he said. "Because I have an idea for a couples costume that I think would be kind of fun. So I will just have to find someone else to dress up with."

I nodded at him, trying to decide what to do. How come I can be a full-fledged adult and still not know how to handle these situations? I decided honesty and sincerity were the best route to take.

"I really am sorry," I said after taking his hand. "I didn't want you to feel like you were second best, but you both asked and then I was really in a pickle. I'm sorry."

"It's alright," Clark said. "Let's just go get a drink or something so we can move past this."

I hopped up into the cab of Clark's truck and he headed towards the Loony Bin, which was the hip bar that everyone our age frequented. Before it came around, there was a sports bar, a veteran's bar, some townie bars and a few bar and grills. This new one, the Loony Bin, was where everyone went for a casual drink. It was nice enough that people dressed up to go there. I had heard a lot about it, but had never actually been there until now.

When we walked in, everyone recognized Clark. They all called "hey!" and waved at him. I got a few hellos also, but not like Clark. We sat down at a little two person table towards the back and I gave him a look.

"What?" he said. "I maybe come here sometimes."

I laughed. I thought it might be more than sometimes, but either way it was fitting for him. A young waiter came over and we each ordered; a glass of white wine for me and an IPA beer for Clark. There was a look of slight horror on Clark's face.

"What's wrong?" I asked, wondering if this had to do with the Halloween costumes again.

"You know what's weird?" Clark said. "I taught that kid in high school and now he's bringing me my beer. It makes me feel pretty old."

I threw my head back and laughed which made Clark laugh a loud laugh also. While I didn't have the same kind of personal connection that he did, it did always make me feel old when I went out and a high schooler was the one taking my order.

I was glad to see that Clark was in a better mood now. I really hadn't expected him to react so sadly, but I was hoping he was over it by now. Judging by how many attractive women greeted him when we came in, he wouldn't have trouble finding someone to dress up with. I just wish those women would hold off on the cutesy talk and touching his arm at least until Clark and I were done with our date.

The waiter brought our drinks and I tried to make more small talk with Clark. As I took a sip of my wine, the front door opened and, judging by the shouts of hello, another regular had walked in. I was surprised to look and see that Candy was the one being welcomed.

She spotted me and made a beeline to the back to say hello. It took her a while because she was continually intercepted for hugs and condolences. It looked like Candy was living the life she had dreamed of in high school. It made me happy for her. I was glad to have a little time to compose myself before she made it to our table.

"Hi Tessa! Hi Clark," she bubbled. "It's so nice to see you here Tess! I mean, I see Clark all the time, but it's a nice surprise to see you."

"I didn't know you were a regular here Candy," I said. I looked her over. She was dressed in a somewhat dramatic, black outfit obviously partially to mourn and partially to catch some attention. Her shirt was so low-cut I was sure I could almost see her navel. She never stopped being Candy.

"Oh yeah, I used to be here all the time," Candy said. "In fact, this is where I celebrated my five year work anniversary with a big party. But I haven't been here for a while because Earl didn't really like to go out very much."

Clark rolled his eyes as he quickly looked away, but I knew what he was thinking. She could try to paint Earl as a good guy with the broadest brush and it wasn't going to fool anyone. But she was a grieving girlfriend and obviously no one was going to argue with her about it.

"Well I'm glad you are here," I said with a smile.

Candy grabbed a chair from a different table and pulled it up between us at our intimate table. The chair didn't quite fit right away, so she just stood there trying to slowly jam it between our chairs until Clark grudgingly got up and moved his chair over to let her in. She grabbed the waiter as he went by and ordered herself a hard cider.

"Did you hear that they arrested someone?" Candy asked. "When I heard the good news, I just had to come celebrate. It's what Earl would have wanted."

I had some serious doubts that Earl would have wanted her to come celebrate with a hard cider wearing a provocative outfit, but I wasn't going to call her on it.

"I heard that you were the one who found the footprint out by the tractor," Candy continued. "So I wanted to thank you for being the one to find the major evidence in this case."

My mind flashed to the watch I had picked up out there. I didn't really know what I was supposed to do with it now, but I felt like I needed to hold onto it for just a little while longer. I suppose it would just live in the little nest I'd made for it in my glove box.

"Oh, well no problem," I said. I was a little flustered because even though I was pretty sure the boot print matched Ralph's boots, I still wasn't sure that Ralph was the killer. It made me feel a little sick to my stomach that it was the evidence I had found that put Ralph behind bars.

Before I had to think of something else to say, the waiter appeared with Candy's drink. She flashed a million watt smile at him while she took a long swig and then turned back to us.

"Well, I really shouldn't keep you," she said. "I can see you are out on a date. I fear it will be too long before I'm on another one of those."

Candy snorted in laughter as she got up and walked back into the crowd of regulars, not bothering to put back the chair she had commandeered. I looked at Clark, who was just as confused as I was.

"Okay, so you thought that was weird too, right?" I asked.

"Ah yeah," Clark said before taking a swig of beer. "Either she is way too happy or she has a super morbid sense of humor."

"Do you think maybe she is just enjoying all of the attention?" I asked. "I know you didn't go to school here, but she was always desperate to be noticed back then. Now she finally is being noticed and I'm going to guess she doesn't want that attention to leave, even if it takes exploiting a death."

"But is she sad at all?" Clark asked.

"I think so," I said, remembering our encounter earlier that day. I told Clark all about her crying over Earl and her story of their argument. It was nice to have an outsider's view on what may have happened. Max was a cop and Mandy was a townie, but I could count on Clark to be a bit more objective about things.

"So it sounds like she is sad," he said. "But also enjoying the attention. I think human beings have space enough to carry around two emotions at once, no matter how strange it may seem."

"You have a point," I said. "But the reason I asked you out is so we could discuss the haunted house, not the murder that might cause all of the plans to fall apart. How is that coming along?"

Clark launched into a gratuitous description of the haunted house he and the students were planning. It seemed like he was almost more excited than they were. I was just glad to be done talking about the murder. It seemed like the murder investigation was done and over with, even if there was something odd that I couldn't quite put my finger on.

•Chapter 18•

The next morning, the front page of the Shady Lake Tribune carried a large picture of Ralph being led into the courthouse along with a smiling byline photo of Chelsea. I'm sure she was thrilled to finally get a front page story that was about something exciting, not just a picture of a tractor or a story about a farmer who grew a giant pumpkin, like the headline the day before had been.

"It'll be nice to finally have this town back to normal," my dad remarked at breakfast. After we served the guests, we always had our breakfast in the kitchen together. My parents usually cooked enough for the guests to have plenty and also to feed the four of us. Unlike some bed and breakfasts, the breakfast at this one was just good old fashioned breakfast food with only a touch of fancy. Today we had scrambled eggs, pumpkin pancakes, and a side of bacon.

"Yeah, I guess," I said. I was tired because it had been really hard for me to fall asleep after hearing about the police bringing Ralph in. I still felt like Ralph wasn't the murderer, but I didn't know who was and I didn't have any evidence besides the watch that I kept checking to make sure was still in my glove box. I just couldn't accept that Ronald had killed Earl. Would·Mayor Panda really do that?

"Tessa, it is your turn to check on the guests," my mother said. While we ate our delicious breakfasts, each of us had to take a turn to check on the guests and make sure they were happy and satisfied. Every fifteen minutes, we would go out and refill coffee and juice and get seconds for anyone that wanted more. After we each did it once, breakfast was generally over.

I stood up and grabbed one more piece of bacon to eat while I headed for the dining room. There was a swinging door that separated the dining room from the kitchen. I grabbed another full coffee carafe in one hand and pushed the door open with my back as I swallowed my last bite.

The dining room table was encircled by the seven guests we had that day. Besides a honeymoon couple that had been here all week, we also had two older, retired couples who were in town visiting their grandchildren, and then there was Susy.

When I walked in, they were all amiably

talking about the Halloween Hayride. The young couple that was staying on their honeymoon had grown up in Shady Lake and were excitedly describing it to the rest of the table. It was always nice to have the same guests for a few days in a row because they would get along nicely without using the conversation cards my parents left in the middle of the table to otherwise facilitate conversation between the guests.

"Would anyone like some more coffee?" I asked, showing them the fresh pot. I checked the carafe in the middle of the table to find it had been drained. The two older couples both indicated they would like more, so I poured them all a fresh cup. Susy's coffee cup was upside down. She must not like coffee very much.

"Tessa here is actually a chair of the Halloween Hayride this year," the young girl said. She was a somewhat familiar face, but I wouldn't have known her name if she hadn't stayed here. Peter could never get used to how people just knew who you were in Shady Lake. He thought it was creepy. I thought it was nice. "Tell us some more about the Hayride. I'm trying to make sure they bring their grandchildren to it."

"We are changing things up a little bit

this year," I said as I poured another cup of coffee. "We will have the same old hayride that we tweak each year. That is perfect for any younger grandchildren. But the most exciting thing this year is a haunted house that is being put on by the high school student council. I just got the rundown on it last night and let me tell you, it sounds terrifying! It'll be perfect for any older grandchildren or maybe even you."

The older couples chuckled and started to make jokes about who was too scared to go in, daring each other to go in. I caught Susy's eye and she was smiling also. For once, it looked like a genuinely, happy smile, even though it only lasted for a fleeting moment. I smiled back at her and she jerked her head towards the hallway as she got out of her chair. I lifted the coffee pot and then put up one finger. Susy nodded, understanding what I meant.

After I switched the coffee carafes and put the empty one back in the kitchen, I met Susy in the hallway. She was pacing back and forth, the happiness gone from her face. It had been replaced by her chewing worriedly on her lip.

"Oh Tessa, I saw the front page of the paper," Susy said when she saw me. "Did they really bring Ralph in? I'm afraid this may have gone too far."

"Yes they did bring Ralph in, but what do you mean it's gone too far?" I asked. "All of the evidence points to him, I'm afraid."

At least, all of the evidence the police have, I thought.

"Well, it wasn't him," Susy said, wringing her hands. "I know it wasn't him, but I can't really tell you how I know that."

"Wait, are you saying you know Ralph?" I asked. "Like you know him besides the fact that he was Earl's crony?"

Susy looked around nervously. She was obviously worried that someone would overhear. My mind was racing, trying to figure out what she could be hiding. I needed to get her somewhere where we could talk without fear that anyone would overhear.

"Let's go get some donuts," I said. I knew Mandy would let us use the kitchen to talk and since it was a weekday morning once the morning rush was done, she would be the only one there.

Susy nodded and before I knew it, we were driving downtown in the station wagon. The Halloween decorations were now out in full force. Besides the Halloween wreaths that had previously been there each streetlight was flying a flag with a picture of a pumpkin on it and garlands of jack o lanterns were strung across the intersections, along with white lights that were lit when it got dark at night. I made a point to take a drive down Main Street every night once the decorations were up.

I parked in my usual alley spot and led Susy in through the back door of the bakery without knocking. Mandy looked up smiling at me, but her face quickly turned to confusion as Susy came in behind me.

"This is Susy," I said. "She has some information about Earl's murder that she wants to tell me, but we need privacy. Can we get that here?"

"Of course," Mandy said. "I'll just be out front stocking the display cases again now that the rush is over."

She grabbed a tray of donuts and pushed her way out to the front of the store. I winked at her as she went, letting her know I would clue her in once we were done talking. I would probably need her levelheadedness to make sure I wasn't jumping to any conclusions.

"Okay," I said. "We're alone. Now spill."

Susy sat down on one of the bar stools

from under the large, metal table that sat in the middle of the room. She took a deep breath and launched into her story. I cleared my head and tried to focus solely on her.

"My uncle was sick for a while before he died," she said. "I had gotten wind of the fact that his will may leave Earl with the business, but I wasn't sure. I knew that if he was put in charge, he would run it into the ground with some of his typical, shady dealings. But I needed some proof. That's where Ralph comes in."

I grabbed two glasses of water and brought over a plateful of donuts I had found. Susy took a long drink of water while I managed to gobble down half a donut. I couldn't resist the siren song of sugar while I waited for her to tell me more.

"Ralph is actually a private investigator that I hired to get information on Earl," Susy said. "So I'm the one that got him into this mess. He would have no reason to kill Earl because then he wouldn't get his final pay, which he desperately needs."

"Why don't you go down and tell the police that?" I asked. It would be simple enough to tell them and they would be able to look into the matter and let him go.

"Because he made me swear not to," Susy

said. "His mother is very sick and he needs the money to pay her medical bills. Ralph doesn't want her to find out what he's been up to because he's had some bad dealings in the past as a PI and his mother made him swear not to take another case. He was desperate and needed the money, but he thinks if he tells his mom, it might cause her enough stress to make her even sicker."

I realized that I had picked up a second donut that I was currently nibbling on. I forced myself to put it back down on my plate and take a big gulp of water instead. I added "drink more water" to my mental list of future New Years resolutions.

The swinging door opened up and Mandy came through carrying two cups of coffee. She set one down in front of each of us. I took a big gulp, wondering if black coffee counted as a cup of hydration.

"Sorry ladies," she said. "I'm all done restocking and needed to pop back here, so I figured I would bring a peace offering."

Susy took one look at her cup of coffee and dashed to the trashcan where she proceeded to vomit up her breakfast. Mandy gave me a look and started to apologize before I held up my hand to stop her. I was pretty sure she might have just helped give me a very large clue. I waited for Susy to come back to the table, where I handed her a napkin and a fresh glass of water.

"I think there is something else you want to tell us," I said.

Susy sat for a moment looking around the kitchen. I could almost see her mentally weighing what she should say next. Finally, she sighed.

"Okay, I can't really deny it now," Susy said. "I'm pregnant. It is still pretty early, though."

"But that's not all, right?" I asked. While Susy had been throwing up, I had finally put the now obvious two and two together.

"No, that's not all," she said. "Ralph is the father."

•Chapter 19•

As I drove Susy back to the B&B, she explained that she and Ralph had fallen in love as he was working on this case and they had just been wanting to wrap everything up so that they could be together for real. But then Susy learned she was pregnant, which is why she had come down to Shady Lake. She had just told Ralph about the baby the morning before the murder. That is why Ralph hadn't been with Earl when I saw him arguing with Candy that morning.

"So on one hand, that could be the motive," I said to Mandy. After I dropped Susy off, I had a strong urge to think through everything I had just learned and Mandy was always ready to lend an ear. I had done a three point turn and headed back to the Donut Hut. Okay, I'd done more like a 10 point turn because the station wagon did not have a very good turn radius. "Ralph could have been tired of Earl's shenanigans and just want to settle down with Susy."

"That's true," Mandy said. "Especially because if they ended up raising a child together, Earl would have figured out their relationship and I get the idea that he wouldn't have been too happy."

"On the other hand," I said. "Would Ralph really risk going to prison for murder and not getting to be in his child's life? I didn't ask how he felt about being a father, but I just don't really think it makes sense either way."

"True," Mandy said as she put two salads down in front of us. The bakery served a limited lunch menu and Mandy had a large chef's salad every day. Somehow she managed to not stuff her face with donuts all day, which is what I know I would do if I worked here. I already do that without being employed at the Donut Hut.

We both munched our lunches in silence for a few moments while Claire, Mandy's part-time lunch waitress came in and out to serve the customers who were here for lunch. I had to admit that Mandy made a pretty tasty salad, even if it didn't really compare to her donuts.

"Maybe we should go over the other suspects," Mandy said. "If we think about each of them, maybe something will become clearer."

"Well, Susy is also a suspect," I said. "She

has the same motive as Ralph and the day after the murder, her car was all dusty and dirty. And let me tell you, she does not seem like the kind of woman who just goes out for a drive on a gravel road."

"But she is pregnant," Mandy said, gesturing with her fork. Somehow she managed to swing it around wildly without throwing droplets of dressing all over the place. "I feel like if she can't even stomach a cup of coffee, she might not be able to murder someone."

I nodded. But running over someone with a tractor felt a little different than stabbing them. That was another point. Did the suburban mom to be know how to operate an old tractor?

"And then there is the watch that we found," I said. "I went in to meet with Ronald about the Hayride a few days ago and his watch was still missing, so it is definitely his. And he admitted to me that he was out at the field that day practicing how to drive the tractor, but he says he left before Earl and Ralph showed up."

"But would Ronald really kill someone to save the Halloween Hayride?" Mandy asked. I could hear the doubt in her voice.

I know we both wanted to think he

wouldn't but he had committed his entire
life to Shady Lake. He allowed himself to be
pied and dunked in the dunk tank to raise
money for the town. He routinely ended up
dressed in dumb costumes to make the
children of Shady Lake happy. But would
that commitment to Shady Lake really
extend to murder?

"There is also Candy," Mandy said,
rolling her eyes. "I can't quite figure her
out."

"Have we ever been able to figure her
out?" I asked. I feel like she hadn't changed
at all since high school, even though we had
all gotten older. She was still desperate for
attention and friends and even though she
was a regular at the Loony Bin, she still
didn't quite fit in.

"Well, she told me she was arguing with
Earl that morning because she thought he
was cheating on her," I said. "He canceled a
date with her and later she heard he was
out with another woman. But she is awfully
broken up about his death, so she obviously
loved him."

I poured myself another cup of coffee. I
offered some to Mandy, but she shook her
head no. She didn't have a love of coffee
like I did. If she had more than two cups a

day, she got all jittery and then her donuts looked weird and everyone thought she drank on the job. It actually happened once and it took Mandy an entire year to convince some people that she wasn't a functioning alcoholic, just someone who was highly sensitive to caffeine.

"Well, what are you going to do?" Mandy asked me. She wasn't there to make a judgment call; she was just the sympathetic ear.

"I'm going to take some time to really figure out what I should do," I said. "I know time is running out, but it is the one thing I need to figure out this case."

Just then, there was a loud knock on the swinging door. Mandy and I looked at each other. Who would knock on the swinging door?

"Yoo hoo," a voice called as the door swung open.

Chelsea appeared through the door with a smirk on her face. She had a pen and notepad in her hand.

"Claire said you two were back here," she said. I could tell by her ultra sweet voice that she was here to schmooze one of us. "I was wondering if I could get a quote for the paper from you, Tessa? After all, you were there to find the body and I haven't interviewed you yet."

"Yeah, why haven't you interviewed me yet?" I asked. Usually Chelsea was practically knocking down doors to interview people, but she hadn't even talked to me yet.

"I was a little busy with Clark," she said with a wink. I wasn't exactly sure I wanted to know what that meant. But I had to admit, it did make me feel a bit of rage, so I hit her right where I knew it would hurt her the most.

"I have no comment for you," I said firmly. "Now, if you would please leave."

Chelsea just smirked as she repacked her notepad into her messenger bag. I could tell she was annoyed, but something was also making her feel vindicated. I figured I would find out that bit soon enough.

"That's fine," she said. "I'll just give Clark a call. You two have a nice day."

She pushed back through the swinging door and a moment later, the bell on the front door rang as she left the Donut Hut. I rolled my eyes. I thought a good journalist tried to report on the story, but Chelsea seemed to try her hardest to insert herself sometimes.

"What do you think that was about?" Mandy asked. She was gathering up our lunch dishes. I grabbed them from her and walked them over to the dishwasher. I wasn't going to make her do all of the dishes after she was the one to make our lunch.

"I have no idea," I said as I loaded a rack of dishes. "You know how she is. She knows Clark and I go out on a few dates and she just wants to try to start drama. But Clark and I both know we see other people and that our relationship is casual. If she wants to date Clark also, she is free to."

"But are you actually okay with that?" Mandy asked. She knew me too well. Sometimes, I could be competitive to a fault.

"Well, I have to be," I said. "I'm not going to raise a big stink seeing as how I've been dating two guys. Although, his choice of Chelsea may make me question his judgment a bit."

Mandy giggled conspiratorially. We tried our hardest to stay out of drama and not be too gossipy, but Chelsea was always determined to try to drag us into it.

After I washed a few racks of dishes as payment for lunch, I jumped back in the station wagon. I needed to take a ride to clear my head a bit. There was still something about this entire murder investigation that was bothering me. Something seemed to be lurking just below the surface. I just hoped it would break through soon so we could solve this and put it all behind us.

•Chapter 20•

The next few days were pretty quiet around town. Things were starting to go back to normal and I was trying to not think about the inconsistencies in the case. Every time I saw Susy, I tried to convince her to go to the police with what she knew about Ralph, but she refused and made me swear not to go either. I figured I would give her a few more days and then make a final decision.

The long postponed tractor driving class was finally going to take place for anyone who wanted to and potentially could drive the tractor for the Halloween Hayride. Clark had asked if I would come to help demonstrate while he taught. I had tried to ask him about Chelsea, but he had just blushed and started stammering, so I had eased up. I didn't really care anyways, or at least I didn't care a lot.

I arrived out at the field shortly before the class was going to start so that Clark could walk me through how he wanted it to go. When I got out of my car, I was a little surprised to see him walking over with a clipboard in hand. I guess I thought he would kind of wing it, but if there was one source of pride in Clark's life, it was his status as a great teacher. I should have figured he probably made a lesson plan for this.

"Hey there," he said with a big smile. "I'm glad you're here this early. I really wanted to run through a few things with you."

I gave him a big hug and breathed in the smell of his cologne. I tried to push the thought of Chelsea breathing in his scent out of my mind. She wasn't going to be here today, so I wouldn't have to worry about her. She knew that the person driving the hayride wouldn't get much attention, so there was no way she would take on that role.

"So I put together a handout," he said, taking a sheet of paper off of his clipboard and handing it to me. I giggled at his thoroughness, but I should have known it was coming.

"Will there be a test at the end of today?" I joked as I poked him in the stomach. I could feel his muscles through his shirt.

Clark laughed, giving me a playful shove. He set his clipboard down on the open tailgate of his truck next to a large disposable bag full of pens and a stack of clipboards so people could take their own notes.

"There will be a test, but only for you," he said. "Don't worry, it'll all be hands on."

He gave me a kiss, a nice, long kiss before pulling back. He ran his hands up and down my back before he stepped back. I bit my lip when it was over, wishing it could go on longer.

"But right now, we need to go over stuff before everyone else gets here," he said, switching over to his serious teacher self again.

We walked together over to where the tractor was still sitting in the middle of the field. I looked around, trying to figure out if it had been moved at all since the murder. Was I gonna have to sit in the hot seat where the murderer had also sat just over a week ago? I shivered at the thought.

Clark obviously thought I was cold, as he put his arm around my shoulders and pulled me closer to him. I appreciated the thought, as the warmth of his body seeped through his down vest and my jacket to bury itself deep inside of me.

"Clark, has anyone actually moved this tractor since it was used to run over and kill a man?" I asked. I had to know. I don't think I would really care one way or the other, but it was the not knowing that was the worst.

"Well, I don't think they actually started it or drove it," he said. "But they pushed it back and forth a little bit to gather, umm, evidence from the tires and stuff."

I shuddered again at the thought of them inspecting the tires for pieces of Earl. I found myself wishing that the murderer had just stabbed or shot him. It wouldn't have been any cleaner, but at least I wouldn't have to think about them scraping Earl off of the tires of the tractor we used to haul around happy, laughing children. Happy Halloween kids!

At least the tractor still looked the same as always and it wasn't surrounded by caution tape anymore. We walked up next to it and stopped. I looked it up and down, half expecting to see something gory, but it just looked like the same old pumpkin colored tractor.

"Okay, so I'll first have you show everyone how to safely climb up onto the tractor," Clark said. I snickered a little bit because there was really only one way to get up on the tractor. Clark frowned slightly at me. Apparently he didn't see the humor in it.

"We need to make sure that we keep safety as an utmost priority," he said, sounding very much like a stern high school teacher. "We don't want anyone else getting run over, do we?"

I shook my head. I certainly didn't want anyone else to get run over. I hadn't even wanted Earl to get run over. I prefer my Halloween Hayrides to be free of any maiming, accidental or otherwise.

"Okay, so show me how you climb up there."

I resisted the urge to roll my eyes at Clark as I turned towards the tractor. I grabbed onto the handle and hoisted myself up to the seat, swinging my leg over the seat to sit down. When I looked down at Clark, he nodded his head at me.

"Okay, now I'd like you to show everyone how to adjust the seat," he said. "It is very important that everyone can drive it comfortably. That will help cut down on potential accidents."

"But what if it is in the right spot for me right now?" I asked. When I sat down in the seat, my feet fit onto the pedals just right. I didn't need to move it at all.

"Well I still need you to show others how to adjust it," Clark said, with a bit of snark in his voice. He continued on explaining the need to properly fit the seat to each individual person, but I had stopped listening to him.

As Clark droned on, I started to have a realization. I glanced around at the entire tractor and then back down at my feet on the pedals. I could feel an idea rising to the surface. It was like a bunch of things were clicking into place until suddenly, the light bulb in my head seemed to go on.

"Wait a minute," I said, interrupting the safety spiel. "You said no one touched the tractor since the murder, right? Like no one touched the seat or drove it?"

"That's what they told me," Clark said with an annoyed look on his face. I assumed he was annoyed at me for interrupting him with what seemed like a trivial question. But to be fair, I was a little tired of his tirade against people who drive tractors with the seat in the wrong position. "Now if we could just…"

"And Ralph is a really big guy, right?" I soldiered on, not letting him continue just yet. I already knew the answer, but I kind of liked playing detective like this.

"Obviously," Clark said, crossing his arms across his chest. "Now what is this all about Tessa?"

"If the last person to drive this tractor was Ralph when he ran over Earl, how come the tractor seat is set for someone my height?" I asked. It was like the heavens had opened up and angels were singing. This was what had looked so odd. This was the thing I just couldn't put my finger on for so long.

Clark's arms dropped to his sides. Instead of trying to push on with his safety lecture, his mouth opened and shut a few times as he tried to think of what to say. I felt the same way, but I had to get proof.

"Clark, do you have your phone on you?" I asked. My flip phone had a camera, but the pictures it took were pretty poor quality. I needed good photos if I was going to prove my point to the police.

Clark pulled out his phone and swiped to bring the camera up on the screen. He lifted it up and I could hear him hitting the shutter button.

"I need you to take a bunch of pictures of me on this tractor," I said. "Take pictures of me on the seat and some close ups of my legs and my feet on the pedals. I want you to take all angles."

Clark dutifully did as I asked. He walked slowly around the tractor as I heard his camera click away. I stayed still as I tried to figure out exactly what this meant. It wasn't like Ralph could have comfortably drove the tractor over Earl and then stopped to adjust the seat to throw everyone off the mark.

"Okay, what do you want me to do with them?" Clark asked after taking pictures from every feasible angle.

"Send them all to my email," I said. "And I hope you don't mind if I skip out on the tractor driving class. I need to show Max these pictures."

"But what do they mean?" Clark asked. I don't think he is really that thick, I think he just hadn't put much thought into the murder. I suppose that besides myself and the police, the only other person who had put much thought into the murder was the murderer.

"It means that they are holding an innocent man for a murder he didn't commit," I said. "And I finally have some proof I can share."

•Chapter 21•

I walked triumphantly into the sheriff's office in the Shady Lake courthouse. Max was standing beside a table that had a coffee pot on it which smelled like it was never actually turned off, simply refilled to make another pot. As he turned to see me, he smiled.

"Well, well, well," he said. "What do we have here? You seem to be cutting the tractor driving class, hmm?"

I smiled back at him. I had only skipped a few classes in high school, but Max had only ever skipped on Senior Skip Day so compared to him, I had been a juvenile delinquent. I used to tease him and call him a goody-goody while he would jokingly call me a rebel.

"I actually have something of great interest," I said. "Do you have a computer I can use?"

Max nodded and led me to his desk. If I had taken the time to glance around the room, I could have picked it out immediately as it was the only desk that was tidy in the whole place. Most desks had some framed pictures or knick-knacks on them. Max's only had a computer, a cup of pens, a phone, a tray for papers, and a nameplate on it. There wasn't even a speck of dust on anything and I got a sudden vision of Max dusting everyday. It would have been funny if I had been certain that it wasn't true.

After pushing the mouse around to wake the computer up, Max pointed to his chair to tell me to sit down. I immediately plopped down and pulled up my email. The top two new emails were from Clark, both with ten attachments each.

"Are you ready for this?" I asked Max. "I am about to blow your mind. I have evidence that Ralph is not the murderer."

"What?" Max said. He actually leaned back from me as he knit his eyebrows together in concern. He looked like he was afraid of catching some sort of disease from me. "Don't joke around. You were the one that found the boot print in the first place. He definitely is the one who did it. He won't actually tell us much of anything. Just give up, the guy is guilty."

I shook my head. There was no way I was going to give up on this. If Ralph was innocent, I wanted to spring him from jail so he could be able to help raise his baby, even though I couldn't really tell Max that.

"First, I have to ask, did anyone sit on or move the seat of the tractor?" I asked. Max just stared at me for a moment. The confusion was obvious on his face.

"No, why would we?" Max finally said. "That wasn't the part of the tractor that ran over Earl. We glanced it over and didn't find any evidence there besides those denim threads."

I clicked on one of the attachments and opened up a photo of me sitting on the tractor. Max raised his eyebrows at me, obviously wondering what this was all about. I could tell he couldn't see what was now so obvious to me.

"How tall would you say Ralph is?" I asked.

"Well over six feet," Max said. There was an undercurrent of annoyance in his voice. Max was used to putting up with my shenanigans, but he didn't have to be happy about it.

"So stick with me, but you would agree that he is around a foot or so taller than me?" I asked. Max nodded his agreement. He still wasn't understanding my point. I would have to spell it out for him.

"Then how come the tractor seat is set for

someone who is my height to drive the tractor?" I asked as I started to slowly click through all of the pictures.

Max sat and stared at me for a beat before he jumped out of his seat and grabbed the mouse out of my hand and started to click through on his own. I scooted the chair back on the wheels and waited. Max started to click even more frantically. He forwarded the emails to himself and then started to save all of the pictures.

"Son of a gun," he whispered to himself as he looked through them for a fourth time. When he got back to the first picture again, he looked at me in admiration. "You're right. How did we miss this?"

I shrugged and stood up out of his chair. He backed up to sit down in it, never taking his eyes off of the screen. It was as if he was afraid the pictures would disappear if he looked away for a moment.

"You missed it because you weren't looking for it," I said.

Max nodded as he picked up his phone and punched in a few numbers. He almost looked like he wanted to pinch himself to make sure he wasn't dreaming.

"Chief, you're gonna want to see this," he said. "Come on out here."

Over the next hour, I explained and re-explained the tractor seat theory to multiple different officers. Each one was more incredulous than the last until they saw the pictures. Once they saw what I meant, each and every one of them looked like they wanted to kick themselves. I couldn't help it if they didn't do a thorough job.

Finally, after I told the same details over and over again, the officers were satisfied that I wasn't a total nutjob and told me I could leave. Max took me by the elbow to guide me out. I think a small part of him was proud of me, even if he would never actually say that to me.

"Well, I'll be a little busy now, thanks to you," he said with a smile. "But I will text you later, okay Sweet Thing?"

I melted a little bit as I smiled and nodded back to him. He winked at me while he gave my arm a little squeeze and walked back into the sheriff's office. I turned the corner to walk back towards where I had parked my car and ran smack into Chelsea, who dropped the stack of papers she had been carrying as she tried to round the same corner.

"Geez Tessa, can't you watch where you are going?"

Chelsea's mouth was twisted into a caricature of a scowl that I'm sure was reserved solely for me.

"Sorry Chelsea," I said as I bent down to help her pick the papers back up. "But I had no idea you were going to walk around that blind corner at the exact same time that I did."

The giant mess of red hair quivered as Chelsea violently shook her head. It made it look like her rage at me was shooting out of the top of her head.

"What are you doing here anyways?" she asked. She made it seem like the courthouse was a private place and it was a total mystery that I could be there. I pondered whether I should remind her that it was a public building. But I came up with a better idea.

"I actually just delivered a tip to the sheriff's office about Earl's murder," I said. I couldn't help but gloat a little bit since Chelsea herself wasn't above a little bragging.

Her face went white as a sheet and her eyes went big. She started to fumble around with her ever present messenger's bag. I'm sure she was looking for some paper and a pen, but one glance in her bag told me she wasn't going to find anything in there very easily. It was stuffed to the gills with crumpled paper and what looked like bits of garbage.

"Will you give me some information?" Chelsea asked as she tried to dig out a pen that was stuck on something I couldn't see in the bag. Her tone had changed rage to desperation. "I can keep it anonymous, if you'd like. Maybe we could go out for coffee and you could tell me everything you know."

As she dug around, the papers she had so carefully gathered were fluttering once again to the ground. I took the stack that I had gathered and put them down on a wooden bench next to where we were standing.

"I'm sorry," I said with a little wave. "But you'll have to get your information from the sheriff's office just like everyone else."

I walked away as I heard Chelsea let out a quiet growl. As I pushed the door open to walk out to the parking lot, I looked back to see Chelsea once again collecting her papers, but this time instead of carefully stacking them in a pile, she was messily crumpling them into a big, untidy stack. Now I understood how her bag ended up in the state it was in.

I couldn't help but smile to myself. If she wanted to rub her relationship with Clark in my face, I found a little bit of pleasure in withholding information from her.

•Chapter 22•

As soon as I got back to the B&B, I felt like my head was spinning. I walked into the library to lay down on the sofa, but when I got there it was already occupied. Susy was sitting on one end of the couch, wrapped in a blanket and reading a book. She looked up and greeted me warmly as I came in.

For a split second, I wondered if I should withhold the news about the tractor from her. After all, she was still on my suspect list. But I knew I had to tell her, if only to set the poor woman's mind at ease.

"I have some good news," I said. Susy scooted her legs and blanket over and I sat down at the opposite end of the couch. For just a moment, I felt almost like we were friends instead of whatever it was we were. "When I went out to the field today to help teach a tractor driving class, I found some key evidence."

Susy's eyes got wide and she quickly sucked in her breath. I realized that she had no idea what the evidence could be and I found it curious that her first instinct was to worry. I wasn't sure if I should take that as a sign that she was guilty or just afraid for Ralph.

"The tractor's seat had not been touched since the murder, but when I climbed up to sit in it, the seat was already set for someone my height. There is no way Ralph could have sat in it to drive the tractor."

A smile slowly crept across Susy's face as she took in the good news. She slammed her book shut and ripped off her blanket, throwing it over the back of the couch. She leaned forward and gave me a quick hug around my shoulders.

"Oh I just knew something would turn up," she said, clapping her hands together. "I was getting so worried that I would have to reveal what I knew to the police. Ralph would have been so mad if I had revealed his secret and obviously I didn't want to tell them that I had seen him drive away from the field while Earl was still out there pacing. I'm so glad you figured this out."

"Wait a minute, what did you just say?" I asked. I had to have heard her wrong. "Did you say you were out there at the field that night?"

"Well, yeah," Susy said. "Ralph had mentioned to me that Earl was planning to go out there that night, so I followed them.

Except by the time I got there, I saw Ralph driving away. I tried to follow him, but my darn morning sickness showed up and I had to pull over to barf again."

"And you say that when you left, Earl was still there?" I asked.

Susy apparently had no idea that she was possibly implicating herself in this murder. She had just admitted to me that she was the last person to see Earl alive.

"When I left, he was down there throwing a fit," Susy said. "He was pacing back and forth, kicking rocks and yelling like crazy. He didn't see me, so I just drove on past."

"Did you see anyone else with Earl?"

"No, like I said, Earl was just down there throwing his little temper tantrum. He was kicking rocks and waving his arms the air and just screaming his little heart out."

That couldn't be right. There had to be someone else down there. We knew that Earl didn't run himself over. So who could it have been? Was Susy implicating herself?

"Thank you so much for doing this, Tessa," Susy was saying. "I'm so grateful that you have helped clear Ralph's name."

I smiled at Susy and got up from the couch. I started to walk out of the living room, but I figured I would warn Susy. I felt a lot closer to her now and I didn't want her to accidentally point the blame towards herself.

"One more thing," I said, turning back to face Susy. "I wouldn't tell anyone what you told me. If you were the last person to see Earl alive, you are going to become the number one suspect."

The color drained from Susy's face as she suddenly realized what she had said and what that could possibly mean. She stood up from the couch and immediately doubled over, grasping the arm of the couch for support. This time she didn't look like she was going to vomit. Instead, Susy looked like she was about to faint.

"I think I need to go lie down," she said quietly.

I put her arm around my shoulders and helped her up the stairs to her room. I tucked her into her bed and put a fresh glass of water next to her.

"Thank you Tessa," she said weakly.

I walked down the stairs, realizing that my mother had asked me to be on desk duty this afternoon. I sat down at the desk and tried to understand the new leads in the case. Ralph couldn't have driven the tractor with the seat where it was. Susy definitely could have, but swears it wasn't her. But she also let slip that she was out there that night. Both Ronald and Candy were about my height, so either of them could still also be the suspect.

This case was as clear as mud. Every time I thought I was clearing things up and getting to the end, I ended up with more questions than answers. Maybe I should be glad I didn't go into police work as a career.

As usual for a mid-afternoon, mid-week shift, desk duty was utterly boring. I played some card games on the computer and answered one phone call. Usually, I would listen to a true crime podcast or something, but I just couldn't right now. I had my own true crime thing going on here. But I tried not to think too much about the investigation because my brain needed a rest. Maybe I was too intertwined in this case, but I couldn't just quit now.

My phone vibrated, cutting through the boredom and silence of the afternoon. I figured it was either Clark asking about the police investigation or Max with an idea for our Halloween costumes, which we still hadn't settled on. Instead, I was surprised to see a message from Candy.

Hey Tessie, I hope I'm not being a bother, but could I bother you for a ride? My car is in the shop and I need to get from the courthouse to my house. I'm just having a hard time today and I need to get home. You're one of the few people I know who is relatively not busy in the middle of the day. Do you think you could help me out?

I was a little weirded out. Did she really not have anyone else to help her? What happened to all of those people at the Loony Bin? But how could I say no to someone who just lost her boyfriend in a still unsolved murder? I decided I would just have to suck up my discomfort and do it.

Okay, I can come drive you. I'll be right there.

I went to find my mother, who was puttering around the B&B tidying up. If there was one thing my mom could usually be found doing, that one thing would be puttering around. If she wasn't actually cooking or cleaning, she was folding laundry, dusting, or even repainting a wall. Puttering was something I hope I would just start doing as I got older. When I found her scrubbing a bathroom faucet with an old toothbrush, I let her know the situation and she assured me that she would watch the desk.

I walked into the town's offices and Candy was sitting at her desk looking pale and sad. She was just staring at her desktop, seeming to look right through the papers sitting on her desk. She really did look like she needed to go home.

I walked up and gently put my hand on her shoulder. She jumped and looked up at me in surprise before relaxing.

"Oh, hello Tessie," she said. I always hated being called Tessie, but Candy had always referred to me by that nickname. I'm not sure why, but it was somewhat endearing coming from her. It was probably because she didn't use it to annoy me on purpose like my siblings did.

"Let's go Candy," I said softly. I helped her up out of her chair and threw her jacket around her shoulders. She managed to pick up her purse and I led her out of the office. I still wasn't sure why she called me, but I was determined to be the friend she needed right now.

●Chapter 23●

Candy was quiet as I helped her get into the passenger seat of my station wagon. I did it as quickly as I could because it was misting out, a cold autumn mist. It was almost, but not quite cold enough to snow so the rain almost felt like little ice pellets. I ran around the front and got in the driver's seat. I started up the car and turned the heater on a little bit higher. The closer it got to Halloween, the colder it got in Minnesota. I usually tried not to turn the heater up too high as the station wagon was pretty old and the heater didn't work well. But I kind of had to when I had other people riding in my car with me.

I pulled out of my parking stall and headed towards the road. I realized suddenly that I didn't actually know where Candy lived. I assumed she didn't still live at her parent's house, but how could I ask her without seeming too awkward. I paused for a while, trying to figure out how to ask her.

"Oh, you probably don't even know where my house is," she said suddenly. I must have paused too long before driving.

"I bought a little yellow house over on Robin Lane. You know where that is, right?"

I nodded. It was sort of by my parent's house, so I just headed in that direction.

"Thank you for coming to rescue me," Candy said. She seemed to have pepped up a bit since leaving the office. "I just got to thinking about Earl and kind of fell into a pit of despair. I heard that they were letting that awful Ralph go! How could they let the murderer go? I just absolutely fell to pieces when I heard that."

"Well actually, I was the one that found the evidence that proved him innocent," I said as I stopped at a stop sign. I wasn't sure why I said that, but I stole a look at Candy. She looked sad and furious, all wrapped up into a little grieving, platinum blond package.

"They can't let an innocent man be punished for a crime he didn't commit," I said gently. I know she was angry, but I hadn't done anything wrong. I wasn't going to let her be mad at me.

Candy huffed and puffed a little bit in the passenger seat. She bit her lip and started to sob a little bit. This car trip was awkward enough and the crying wasn't helping. I

wasn't really sure how to comfort a high
school acquaintance that I hadn't seen in a
decade or so.

We rolled up to her street and Candy
pointed for me to turn right. I put on my
turn signal and made sure no one was
coming. Ever since Peter's accident, I was
always very conscious of driving safely and
especially of the importance of turn signals.

"It'll be on the right side of the street,"
she said through her tears.

Finally, I saw a little yellow house and,
assuming it was hers, I pulled up to the
curb outside of it. Candy looked over and
nodded that it was indeed her house. By
this point, the tears were streaming down
her cheeks.

"Do you have any tissues?" she managed
to ask through her sniffles. She wiped her
nose on the back of her hand. "Maybe in
your glove compartment?"

Before I could stop her, she opened up the
glove compartment and started to rummage
around. She pulled out a wad of tissues and
grabbed one off of it. I watched in horror as
the watch seemed to unwrap itself in slow
motion from the wad of tissues. Candy blew
her nose loudly into the tissue she had
pulled off and then froze as she noticed the

watch.

"Is that what I think it is?" she said, the snotty tissue frozen in her hand in midair. She stared at the watch in the glove compartment, unblinking. For a moment is was like neither of us could even breathe.

I couldn't lie to her. She was Ronald's secretary. I wondered if she had noticed that Ronald's watch had conveniently been missing and here it was in my glove box. There was no lie I could come up with that would even come close to making sense.

"Yes," I said. "It's Ronald's watch. I found it out at the field near the tractor the day after Earl was murdered."

Candy's face had an odd expression on it that I couldn't quite pin down. She sat motionless, staring at the watch with the tissue still held a few inches from her face. She kept squinting and wrinkling up her nose.

"I hid it because I didn't want to implicate Ronald," I said. "I just can't imagine Ronald did it. So I hid the watch in my glove compartment and I've been trying to figure out what to do with it ever since."

"Well I did notice at one point that Ronald was missing his watch," Candy said slowly. "But I didn't think anything of it.

Do you really think that he could be the murderer?"

"Honestly, I just can't," I said. I pictured Ronald sitting in his office playing with his little Halloween toys and munching on his clandestine candy corn all while clad in a sweater vest. That just wasn't the picture of a murderer in my mind.

As we sat with the warm air blasting out of the vents, the rain outside started to pick up. We both sat in silence staring at the watch as the rain plinked on the car roof. I wondered if I should try to ask her to keep it on the down low? But her boyfriend had been the one killed. She wasn't going to withhold key evidence just because I asked her to.

"Earl did mention that Ronald had been threatening him," Candy said quietly. "Ronald had been mad that Earl had mentioned being paid for the Halloween Hayride. I mean, after all, he was basically letting them rent the land for free. Didn't he deserve some compensation? But Ronald didn't think so."

I didn't think he deserved compensation for the Halloween Hayride at all and obviously his uncle hadn't either. But I couldn't believe that Ronald would threaten him over it. When Earl had burst into the planning meeting before he was killed, Ronald hadn't been the one to stand up to him, Clark had. Ronald had seemed honestly more put out and confused than angry. He had been the one trying to keep the peace between everyone.

"I'm just saying that Earl told me Ronald had threatened him," Candy said, shrugging her shoulders. "And now Ronald's watch was found at the scene of the crime. I think it all just adds up too neatly."

I nodded. Was I just blinded by the fact that I'd known Ronald for so long? Or that he was so intertwined with life in Shady Lake? Maybe I was just as bad as one of the townies of looking past one of our own, thinking I knew them better than I did.

"I can't tell you what to do, Tessa, but I can tell you what I think you should do," Candy said. She covered the watch up with the tissues and pushed it back into the mess of the glove compartment. She pushed it shut with a click and looked at me. Her eyes were strangely blank. I think the day had been too much for her.

"I think you should turn that in," Candy continued. She was talking slowly, a far cry from how emotional she had been when I picked her up from work. "You turned in the evidence that let Ralph loose. I think you have an obligation to turn in some evidence that could show them who the real killer is."

She opened the heavy car door and stepped out into the rain. Candy bent down and looked into the car at me one last time. Her eyes seemed to bore right through me.

"Thank you for the ride," she finally said as she shut the car door and ran into the little, yellow house.

I hated to admit it, but I think she might be right. I had to turn in the watch.

•Chapter 24•

"So what you're telling me is that you found a vital piece of evidence at the scene of a murder and you picked it up and hid it?" Max asked.

We were sitting in my warm station wagon as the rain poured down. After I made sure Candy had gotten into her house, I sent Max an SOS text, telling him to meet me in the courthouse parking lot because it was an emergency and to bring an evidence bag with him. I knew I needed to give the watch to him before I chickened out and decided to keep the watch to myself.

"Well, when you say it like that, it sounds a lot worse than what I thought I was doing," I said. I squirmed in my seat. I really hadn't meant to hide evidence, but looking back, that is exactly what I did. I really just thought I had been doing what I needed to do to help Ronald and Shady Lake

"You could get in a lot of trouble for this, Tessa," Max said. "But I'll do what I can to shield you from it."

I looked into his eyes and knew that he

was telling the truth. Those blue eyes were the same I had gazed into during our puppy love days in high school. Now here we were as full-fledged adults and just like back then, Max was helping to keep me out of the trouble that I managed to create. Life always manages to circle back around.

"I'm so sorry to put you in this position," I said. "But thank you. Thank you times a million."

Max took my hand and lifted to his mouth. He kissed the back of it gently, his lips were warm against my cold hands. He tenderly kissed each fingertip before wrapping both of his large hands around my hands. We sat for a few minutes, frozen in time as the rain poured down onto the station wagon. I wanted to sit in our little bubble forever, where we wouldn't get in trouble for me hiding evidence.

"I will always be there for you Sweet Thing," he said. And I knew he meant it.

Max leaned forward and gave me a quick kiss on the lips before climbing out of my car. I watched his back retreating quickly into the courthouse through the falling rain and I wondered what he would do. I suppose he would just have to say he found it from some anonymous tip. I hoped that I hadn't just gotten him into a load of trouble.

I debated whether I should go home, but as far as I knew, I didn't have to work today. Instead, I drove to the Donut Hut and parked in the alley. Before I got out of my car, I sent a quick text to Candy to let her know that I had turned the watch in to Max. I got a message back right away that just said:

Good. Thanks for doing the right thing.

I wasn't sure I had actually done the right thing, but at least it would help put Candy's mind at ease. I dashed from my car to the back door of the Donut Hut and pushed my way into the warm kitchen. As always, it was warm and inviting, filled with delicious smells. I took off my wet jacket and hung it by the door. Even though I was only out in the rain for a few moments, it was raining so hard that my jacket was cold and soaking wet.

Mandy was standing at the counter, pouring glaze over some fresh donuts. Her apron was spattered with flour and she even had some in her dark hair. I loved watching Mandy make donuts because she was totally in her element as she did it. As I came in, she smiled at me and nodded towards the coffee pot.

"Will you pour me a cup too?" she asked. She knew that coffee was always my first priority when I came in.

I poured two cups of coffee and set one next to her on the metal island while I sat down and sipped mine. The hot coffee spread warmth throughout my body as I drank it, driving out the chilliness in my bones that the cold rain had seemed to set in deep. I wrapped my hands around the hot cup and let the coffee inside warm up my freezing cold fingers.

"Mandy, I may have just done something bad," I said after a few drinks. "I need you to set my mind at ease."

Mandy stopped what she was doing and looked me up and down with one eyebrow arched. She took a sip of coffee before she spoke.

"Okay, I give up," she said. "Tell me what you did."

I paused for a moment. I felt so bad about turning in the watch even though I had to. I felt guilty, but I still had to tell Mandy. She had played a part in finding the watch. Mandy let me sit for a few moments in silence before I finally spilled the details of what I did.

"I gave the watch to Max just now," I

said. "And told him about how Ronald was missing his watch. I told him I thought the watch I had found was the one Ronald was missing."

"You what?" she said. Her eyebrows furrowed and her dark eyes burnt into me. It wasn't often that I surprised Mandy with something I did. We were so alike that we could usually predict each other's moves before we did them.

"Sit down and I'll explain," I said, pulling out another stool for her.

I poured more coffee and wrapped both of my cold hands around my hot cup for some comfort. Then I proceeded to tell her the whole story. I told her about going to pick up Candy from work after she sent me a message and how distraught she was about Ralph being let go. I told her about how Candy had accidentally found the watch in the glove compartment while she was looking for tissues and how I couldn't lie to her about it because she seemed to know what it was. And then I told her what Candy had said about Ronald threatening Earl.

Mandy sat on her stool, quietly sipping coffee and listening to the whole story. One thing I always appreciated about Mandy was her ability to just sit and listen without interjecting her thoughts and feelings. Even her face was neutral, which made it much easier to tell about giving the watch to Max, since I wasn't even sure yet that it had been the right thing to do.

"Well, I understand why you turned the watch in," Mandy said when I was done talking. "It's not like you could withhold evidence forever. But I have to agree that I'm still not sure whether it was the correct thing to do or not. I just don't believe that Ronald could have done it. I don't even believe he ever threatened Earl, no matter what Candy says happened."

I raised my mug to my lips and breathed in the bitter smell before I took a big gulp. The coffee was warming me up and calming me down.

"You know that I feel the same way," I said. "I'm not sure I believe Candy, but if Ralph didn't do it, who did? I'm so confused. I feel like everything is staring me dead in the face and I just can't make sense of it."

"If it makes you feel better, I'm not sure you had any other choice," Mandy said quietly. "You couldn't lie to Candy about it. And you know that at some point, you had to do something with the watch. It couldn't just stay in your glove compartment forever."

I felt so much better. Mandy had a way of reassuring me that no matter what, I had done what I thought was best. She gave me one more knowing look and stood up to go back to her work. I stayed on the stool, slowly finishing up my last cup of coffee.

One thing I had learned since moving back to Shady Lake was that it was never a bad idea to go see Mandy at the Donut Hut, even though it was pretty bad for my waistline.

•Chapter 25•

After turning in the watch, I tried to push all thought of the murder investigation out of my mind. I had other things to worry about, things that I had been procrastinating on because I was just so focused on investigating. The Halloween Hayride was starting on Friday and while my role as marketing chair meant making sure that flyers were in the appropriate places in town and that the newspaper was printing our ad and columns about the Hayride, I had also been put in charge of finding a few, fun activities to have available for kids while they waited for their turn on the Hayride. So far, I hadn't even thought about what I wanted to do for the activities, even though I had less than a week to get them together.

Not only was I making sure everything was ready for the Halloween Hayride, I was also in charge of planning some fun, seasonal breakfasts for the B&B along with decorating the common areas and front porch for Halloween. I had put up a few of our more "strictly fall" decorations on October first that we put up every year, so it wasn't like I had done nothing. But I hadn't come up with anything new and I hadn't thought of seasonal breakfasts either.

My mother, Teri, had never been a fan of Halloween. Christmas? She was gung-ho to decorate and celebrate after Thanksgiving was over, just like I was. But she could take or leave Halloween. She didn't like anything about pumpkins besides how cute they were. She didn't like anything scary or creepy. And she just didn't see the thrill of dressing up. So this year, my mother was thrilled that I was around and would be happy to do the planning for this specific holiday.

But if I'm honest? I totally forgot that I'd promised to do more until this week. So most of my desk duty was used to search online for recipes and cute and modern ways to decorate. This was the only time I was thankful my mother wasn't a Halloween fan because she preferred if our Halloween decorations only made an appearance for a few days as opposed to the month long residency that our Christmas decorations had every year.

I was knee deep in stylishly cobwebbed mantles and pumpkin spice pancakes when my phone rang. I flipped it open to see

Ronald's name on the caller ID. My stomach started turning and I felt like I was about to throw up. Did he find out that I had sort of ratted him out? I went back and forth about whether I should answer, but just as it was about to go to voicemail, I hit the green button.

"Hey there Ronald," I said, trying to sound casual. I was totally using my fake, retail happy voice but Ronald didn't seem to notice.

"Tessa, I don't have much time," he said. His frantic voice seemed to drill deep into my consciousness. "The police will be here momentarily to bring me in and I just need to make sure that you are prepared to officially take over the Halloween Hayride. No matter what happens to me, I need to know that the Hayride is safe."

"I promise you that I will make sure the Hayride is a hit," I said. I let out a silent sigh of relief. Obviously he had no idea that I had a hand in him being brought in. But immediately afterward a feeling of intense guilt settled over me. I was the one who had caused this.

"Thanks so much Tessa," he said. He sounded visibly relieved. Leave it to Ronald to be more worried about the Halloween

Hayride than the fact that he was going to jail. In my mind, that was a tally in the innocent column for him. "That puts my mind at ease."

In the background, I could hear Melinda yelling at him to put the phone down and come help her figure out what she was going to do while he was away. Any other man would probably find jail to be a break from a woman like Melinda, but poor Ronald would miss her while he was away. In a way, it was sweet. I always felt it was a testament to true love.

"I have to go," Ronald said. "Hopefully I'll talk to you again soon Tessa."

I flipped my phone shut and laid my head down on the desk. The guilt felt like it was pushing me down hard into the desk. I kept trying to remember what Mandy had said. I knew I would have to do something with the watch at some point. I was just really hoping that what I would do with it would be to give it back to Ronald after the murderer had been found and arrested. Looking back, that was a totally delusional thought on my part.

My phone buzzed again, this time with a text instead of a call. I opened it back up, afraid I'd see Ronald's name as the sender. I didn't think I could handle another conversation with Ronald.

Instead, the message was from Max. That made me feel a little bit better, but also just brought up the fact that we still had not decided on Halloween costumes even though Max had been bugging me about it for a week now. As proof his latest message simply read:

Halloween Costumes???

I cringed a little and opened a new tab on the computer to search for costume ideas. I was getting to the point of telling him to wear all red and I'd wear all yellow and we would just go as condiments. That had always been my go to just in case I didn't think of anything else. Peter had always thought it was a totally ridiculous idea, but it always meant he was the one that figured out what we were going to dress up as.

I scrolled through pages of search engine results for couples costumes, but every time I found something cute, it looked like the costume would take a number of hours to make or was something I'd have to order that probably wouldn't get here in time. Even if I hadn't been busy trying to nosily solve a murder that I wasn't supposed to, I didn't have the time to make some of these costumes.

Finally, I closed the costume tab and just made up my mind that next year, I would start earlier and do a better job. Max was just as indecisive as I was, so I finally made the executive decision and sent him a message.

Alright Max, I'm gonna level with you. We are both busy people. You find a red outfit and I will find a yellow outfit. I'll print off some signs and we can go as ketchup and mustard.

I grimaced as I pressed send, remembering how dumb Clark had thought that idea was. I mean, it was kind of a dumb idea. But it was the best I had and I was pretty sure no one else would be dressed like that. It wasn't a costume idea I was particularly excited about, but it was cheap, easy, and not over done. My phone buzzed again.

Well, that's certainly different. But I guess it'll work. We will have to try harder on a costume next year.

My heart skipped a beat. Even though both Max and I had agreed that we were just seeing each other casually since neither of us was ready for a serious relationship yet, it was still heart melting to hear that he thought we'd be dressing up together again next year.

I opened a new tab and typed "ketchup mustard costume signs" into the search engine. I was sure I'd find something that would look a whole lot better than anything I could make on the fly. Now, my only problem would be finding yellow pants.

•Chapter 26•

The next morning, I was saddened but not surprised to see Ronald on the front page of the Shady Lake Tribune as he was led into the courthouse in handcuffs. It made me a little mad that they had put him in handcuffs. It wasn't like Ronald was going to be much trouble. As we sat together to eat breakfast in the kitchen, my dad read the story out loud. I tried to not visibly wince as he got to the part about the watch being found on account of an anonymous tip. My dad glanced at me, trying to read my expression, but I remained as neutral as I possibly could. I felt bad enough about what happened. I didn't need my father to pile more guilt on top of it.

"I can honestly say I never saw that coming," my mother said as she sipped her tea. Once my parents had retired, my mother decided she needed to take up drinking tea because otherwise she'd be drinking coffee all day and would probably never sleep again because she'd be up using the bathroom all the time. I'm not really sure what is different about her tea drinking habit, but I didn't bother asking. I get my coffee drinking habits from her, including a cup of decaf with my dessert every night.

"Ronald always seemed like such a gentle man," my mom said. "I can't imagine why he would have killed Earl."

"Well, I think we understand why," my father said. "Earl was a terrible, terrible person. Not that I think that anyone should be murdered or anything. I also think that Ronald still is a gentle man. I think the police may be grasping at straws a bit. This is already the second suspect they've brought in that they were sure did it."

I quietly focused on eating my eggs and bacon. I nodded along and just made some noises of agreement so that hopefully they wouldn't ask me my opinion. I really didn't want to talk about the investigation. I'd put enough thought into it and it was at a point where I didn't think I could do anything else even though I thought the police had it wrong.

"As long as it doesn't ruin our haunted house," Tank grunted into his cereal. Despite the amazing breakfasts my parents cook for us and the guests, Tank was a typical teenager who after devouring more than his share, still needed a giant bowl of sugary cereal for his breakfast. Sometimes I wondered if I should buy him some sort of vacuum attachment we could affix to his face for even more proficient food consumption.

"I'm sure your haunted house will go on just as planned," I said. "In fact, since I am the one in charge of the Hayride now, I know it'll be just fine. Now if you'll excuse me, I need to go check on the guests."

Tank rolled his eyes at my statement. I ignored it, slurped down the rest of my coffee and stood up from the table. My mother and Tank were somewhat oblivious, but my father gave me a pointed look. Anyone else would've just thought he had an itch on his face that he was trying to be rid of by arching his eyebrow, but growing up with him, I recognized a look of doubtfulness when I saw it.

I pushed through the swinging door with the coffee carafe, a routine I repeated every morning. This time, though, an accused murderer that I had cleared was also sitting at the dining room table. Ralph had moved into Susy's room after he was released from jail because they were both told they needed to hang out in Shady Lake until everything was totally settled.

The mood around the breakfast table was much more subdued than the happy chatter that I had found on previous mornings. There was a copy of the Shady Lake Tribune on the table with Ronald's face staring up at everyone, but everyone was ignoring it and from it's pristine condition, I got the feeling that no one had dared to even touch it this morning.

I made the rounds, quietly filling cups and checking to see if anyone needed more food. When I got to Ralph's spot, he grabbed my sleeve as I finished filling up his coffee cup. He pulled me down a little bit closer to him.

"Tessa, I heard you were the one who got me released," he said quietly. "I just wanted to thank you. From the bottom of my heart, thank you so much. I, I mean we, are forever indebted to you."

Ralph looked straight into my eyes and squeezed my hand before looking towards Susy. Susy looked at him with such a look of love that I almost shed a tear. I was glad to see that some good did come out of this situation, even if I still felt guilty.

"You're welcome," I said. It was the only thing I could say. This situation just felt like it was spiraling out of everyone's control.

First Ralph had been the suspect and I wasn't sure if he was or not, but I helped clear him. Now Ronald was the suspect that I helped implicate, even if I wasn't sure it was him either. I needed to clear my head.

As usual, I drove myself to the Donut Hut. I parked in my usual alley spot, but I wasn't sure I wanted to see Mandy all by myself. I had a feeling that she had some words for me and I was feeling guilty enough as it was. So I pushed open the front door and waved to the regulars as I walked up to the counter. I had to plaster a fake smile on my face, because every table I went past had a copy of the Shady Lake Tribune on it with that same picture of Ronald staring up at me. Everyone was absolutely buzzing from the news of Ronald being brought in as the main suspect in the murder.

There was already one person waiting for their donut and, judging by the mop of red hair, it was someone I didn't really want to see.

"I'm just so glad I was there to get the picture last night," Chelsea was telling Mandy over the counter as I walked up. "If I keep getting these front page stories, I might just be able to work my way up to a bigger newspaper."

"I highly doubt blurry pictures and a cobbled together story will make you a famous journalist," I said. Chelsea whirled around and Mandy glared at me even though I know she was thinking it too. My big mouth got me again. I kicked myself a little, wondering why I never learn from my mistakes.

"Oh that's rich, coming from someone who couldn't make it in the big city and had to come running home to mom and dad," Chelsea said. She gave me one more stink eye and then turned back to Mandy. "Give me my donut please. I'd rather not hang around with someone who can't spot real talent."

Sometimes, I'm not sure how Mandy can keep a straight face, but she did as she handed Chelsea a chocolate, glazed donut wrapped in a piece of wax paper. Chelsea stomped past me to the front door, giving me a look that would have been accompanied by a stuck-out tongue if we'd been in elementary school.

"Tessa," Mandy said. She had a way of saying my name in a motherly tone of voice that just chilled me to the bone sometimes. I tried to play the innocent act, but it didn't work. She could always see right through me.

"Okay, so I'm feeling pretty bad this morning," I said. Mandy put a frosted cake donut on a plate and slid it across the counter to me. She always knew how to make me feel better. Food was her love language.

"Go sit down over there and I'll bring you a cup of coffee," she said. Mandy smiled just enough to show that she wasn't upset with me.

I walked over to the same table I had stealthily interrogated Ralph at. It was hidden away in a corner, perfect for watching everyone else and hiding from them at the same time.

A few moments and half of a donut later, Mandy walked over with two steaming, white ceramic mugs in hand. When she sat down, we spent a few moments just drinking coffee, not just talking. I had a briefly wondered how long we spent in life doing this exact thing: sitting at the Donut Hut drinking coffee and eating donuts. I'd love to see how many hours we passed together like this when I got to the end of my life.

"It isn't your fault," Mandy said finally.

"Yes it is," I said. "Who else's fault would it be? I turned in the watch and now Ronald has been arrested."

"It isn't your fault because all you did was turn in a piece of evidence that you found at a crime scene," Mandy said. "You did exactly what you should have done."

"Well isn't that a first," I muttered before I drained the rest of my coffee.

Mandy gave me a pointed look.

"The only other choice you had was to hide evidence that possibly implicated a murderer," Mandy said quietly. "I don't really think that would be the best choice."

I nodded. I looked over at my friend and thought about how great it is to have a lifelong friend. Mandy saw things in me that I never would and she was not afraid to tell me the good and the bad. I don't know what I would do without her.

•Chapter 27•

"I thought for sure we'd be able to find red and yellow pants here," Max muttered. We were at the second hand store and we had only been there for three minutes, but apparently Max had expected the right pants to just magically fly off of the rack and into our hands.

I rolled my eyes at him and kept scanning the racks for anything acceptable to add to our condiment costumes. We had already been to a regular store and found our red and yellow shirts but nothing to wear on the bottom half, so here we were shopping second hand. Now, I love second hand shopping. My mother and I love to come down here on a Saturday morning and just scan through the racks to find some gems. But it was a little different when you came looking for something very specific.

The only hard part was that besides a very basic organization, everything was just thrown onto racks. They separated clothing into mens, womens, or children and then they divided tops from bottoms. So when you wanted to look for something very specific, you had to go to the general section and just start digging.

And that is exactly what I had done. Max and I had started in the men's clothing looking for a pair of red pants. And we were certainly finding red pants, but not the right kind of red. All of the red pants we had pulled out so far were more of a maroon color, which was definitely not right for a ketchup costume.

"Ah ha!" Max said, as he triumphantly pulled a hanger out of the depths of a clothes rack. A pair of bright red athletic pants were draped over it.

"Now the real test," I said. "Are they the right size?"

Max grabbed them off of the hanger and held them up to himself. They were a little long, but otherwise looked like they would work around the middle.

"I'll just roll up the bottoms," he said. "Now to try to find you some yellow pants."

We walked over to the women's section. This was going to be a challenge. I figured we could find red bottoms because Shady Lake High School's colors were red and blue. Actually, we called the school colors "cherry" and blue and while there wasn't much of a distinction between cherry and red, we made sure to always say cherry and blue.

Yellow, on the other hand, was not going to be anywhere as prevalent. Just a glance around showed a very distinctive lack of yellow anywhere in the women's section. I half wondered if someone who really loved yellow had already been in and snatched up everything they could find.

"So, how is Ronald doing?" I asked. I'd been wondering if I dared bring up the investigation, but Max seemed to be in a good mood, so I decided to risk it.

"Oh, he is doing fine, all things considered," Max said. I wasn't sure if he was just really busy looking for the elusive yellow pants or if he didn't want to tell me much.

"Yeah? Whatever happened with the watch?" I asked. I tried to look casual as I flipped through the clothing.

Max shot me a look. It seemed like he was weighing whether he should tell me something important or not. I quietly kept leafing through the clothing, pretending not to notice him glancing at me.

"Ronald claims the watch isn't his," Max said. "He says that yes, his watch is missing but no, that one isn't his and no, he can't tell us what happened to his watch."

If Ronald had known where his watch was, why didn't he get it and put it on when I had pointed out it was gone? Yet another piece of information to file away.

"Well, does that one I found fit him?" I asked. "Maybe it isn't his watch."

"That's sort of the problem," Max said. "When people at City Hall get their watch, they just get a standard watch. It isn't sized for them and it isn't personalized. The jewelry store just keeps a couple in stock for whenever another one is needed. So technically that watch could belong to anyone who has worked at City Hal for more than five years."

I nodded at Max and tried to keep up my casual act, but inside a wave of relief rushed over me. Maybe Ronald hadn't done it. Had he been framed then? Or was the killer still out there somewhere in hiding?

Max cleared his throat suddenly and I startled. I got the feeling that I'd been standing there staring at nothing like an idiot while I thought through the implications of the mystery watch.

"Okay Detective," he said with a sly smile on his face. He walked over to stand next to me. "Don't take this as a sign you need to take up the case or anything."

I elbowed him playfully in the ribs. He could read me like a book. Between Max and Mandy, I could never keep anything secret.

"I do want to ask you one more thing," I said. I had a chance and I was going to seize hold of it and milk Max for all of the information I could get. "Do you think it is Ronald's watch or do you think he is lying? I want to know what you personally think, not what the police are thinking."

Max sighed and bit his lip. He stopped looking at the clothing racks and turned to face me. He took my hand in his. I was always a little bit surprised by how soft his large hands were.

"What I am going to tell you is strictly between us and I'm only telling you because you trusted me to give the watch to," Max said quietly. I nodded, hoping nothing would break the spell that had apparently been cast over us in this moment.

"I really want to believe that he didn't do it," Max said. "I've known Ronald for years just like you and I just don't think this is something he would ever do. But what else am I supposed to think when he admits he doesn't have his watch and won't tell us anything about it?"

"That's understandable," I said.

"The other thing is that when we first brought him in, the first thing he said was that he had been down at the field earlier in the day, but he couldn't tell us where he actually was during the murder," Max said. "He said that it was possible we would find his DNA or something because he had been down there practicing with the tractor, but he said he has an alibi that he can't tell us. I've gone round and round with him because that's not really an alibi then, is it? But he just won't say what he was doing that night."

What in the world could be so bad that Ronald didn't want to tell police about? What could be worse than being charged with murder? I wondered if it was something he was keeping from Melinda. The only thing Ronald was more devoted to than Shady Lake was his crotchety wife.

"Hey, look what I found," Max announced. He triumphantly pulled a bright yellow pair of wind pants out of the rack. They looked about three sizes too big, but I could cinch them up until they fit. Judging from the lack of anything else yellow, they would have to do.

"Score!" I said. "They'll have to work."

Max looked very proud of himself and his find. He did a little dance while he waved them around to show off that he'd been the one to find them. Clark would never think of doing something so silly, but I loved seeing Max's silly side.

We brought our purchases up to the counter to pay for them. We spent a grand total of $1.50 on the purchase of our costume bottoms. Really, the only thing we had left to do was to find the signs we would print off to wear. I had already downloaded a few options, so I just had to make my choice and print them off. If I was feeling really into it, I would maybe even laminate them.

Max needed to get to work soon, so he drove me the long, winding way around the lake while we held hands, just like in high school. We had spent a lot of time in high school clipping the lake with the music blasting, although a lot of times we had Mandy along in the back seat. Somehow having her along never felt like having a third wheel.

I tried to focus on the here and now while we wound our way to the B&B. I looked at the beautiful colors of the trees and tried to think about how much I love autumn. But instead I kept thinking about why in the world Ronald wouldn't come clean about his alibi.

•Chapter 28•

Ralph was sitting by himself in the front room of the B&B when I got home from my mid-day date with Max. Maybe he had some information about Ronald and what in the world was happening. After all, he kind of owed me.

"Hey there," I said as I came in. "Can I get you a drink?"

"Oh sure," he said. "Any sort of cola would be great."

I went to the kitchen and grabbed a can of pop for Ralph and a glass of lemonade for myself. I walked the tray of beverages back to the living room where Ralph was sitting on the couch, staring out the window. My father had filled the yard space outside of the living room with bird feeders, a bird bath, and bird houses. Sometimes I wondered if he had maybe gone a little overboard with the bird stuff, but it worked. There were always birds coming and going, sometimes blue jays and cardinals, but also a lot of chickadees.

"Thanks for the drink," Ralph said. "You know, one of the things I missed while I was in jail was pop. They only let me drink water and then a little cardboard carton of milk at meals. But a cola really hits the spot."

For a while, we sat in silence and enjoyed our beverages while we watched the birds. I couldn't imagine being in jail and not being able to enjoy something as simple as a pop. I wondered if they could drink coffee in jail. That brought my thoughts back to Ronald. I just couldn't imagine what he was hiding that was so important.

"I have a few questions to ask you about the night of Earl's murder," I blurted out. I hadn't even really thought through my questions, but it was now or never thanks to my big mouth.

Ralph set his can down on the end table and turned to look at me. His eyes searched my face, looking for something. I wasn't sure what he was looking for, but he must have found it.

"You know, I would tell anyone else no," he said. "But you were the one who helped get me out of a bind. So yes, I will answer a few questions for you."

I took a sip of lemonade to stall for a moment while I figured out exactly how I wanted to proceed with questioning. I mean, I had a bunch of questions I wanted to ask him, but I couldn't just sit here all afternoon peppering him with annoying, dumb questions.

"I guess my first question would be if you saw Ronald out at the field at all that day," I said. I needed to make sure I focused on questions about Ronald because I knew most of the other details. What was important right now was to clear Ronald's name.

"Sure, we saw him out there," Ralph said. "When we pulled up, Ronald was just getting in his car. He had just put the tractor away and was locking up when we came by and told him not to bother. He wasn't very happy about it, but technically it is Earl's land and stuff so he did as Earl said."

"Was he upset?" I asked.

"I haven't known Ronald long at all, at least compared to all of you town people," Ralph said. "But he seemed as mad as he ever gets. He was more flustered and his face turned red. He was huffing and puffing about not letting Earl get away with ruining the Hayride."

"Was he threatening Earl?" I asked. I really hoped the answer was no.

Ralph took a long drink of pop and together we watched a bird eat a few sunflower seeds before flying away. Birds were amazing to watch sometimes. They were beautiful creatures and if everyone would just take a few moments out of their day to watch them, I think it would solve a lot of stress problems in this world. A love of bird watching was yet another thing I got from my father.

"I want to say that he wasn't threatening Earl," Ralph finally said. "But he definitely was. He wasn't like outright telling him to watch his back, but in his Ronald way, he was letting Earl know that there was no way he would let Earl destroy a town tradition like the Hayride."

I sipped my lemonade a little bit more. That definitely made it trickier to prove Ronald wasn't the killer if he had been threatening the victim mere hours before the murder along with all of the other evidence they had already collected.

"Did you tell all of this to the police?" I asked.

Ralph nodded slowly with a grimace on his face. I had expected that. He had no reason to withhold that information, of course, but it would have made my life a lot easier if he had.

"I have one more question, if that is

alright," I said. Ralph looked at me for a moment and then nodded once.

"Did you see anyone else around?" I asked. "Anyone at all? Any cars or anything at all?"

Ralph thought for a moment.

"I know the police probably asked you this question and that it might be very obvious," I said.

"Actually, they did ask me, but they only asked if I saw anyone," Ralph said. "They didn't seem to care if I saw any vehicles or anything. I did see a car in my rearview mirror as I drove away from the field. But I can't quite remember what kind of car it was."

I sat up straighter as he talked. This was the kind of lead I needed, even if it was extremely vague. Someone had shown up just after Ralph left. Susy had mentioned trying to follow them that night. Had Ralph just implicated her?

"Was the car you saw Susy's SUV?" I asked.

"What? No," Ralph said, looking genuinely confused. "I would know if it were Susy's car. Why would you think it was her?"

"She previously mentioned being out

there that night," I said. "I just wondered if maybe you saw her car."

Ralph shook his head a few times before taking a long drink of his pop. He could be lying, I guess, but he seemed genuinely befuddled by my suggestion.

"No, I would have definitely known her car," Ralph said. "And if I saw her car, I would have gone back. I wouldn't have let her face Earl alone."

"I'm going to give you my phone number," I said. "If you remember absolutely anything about the car, I want you to let me know."

I ran to the desk and jotted my phone number as legibly as possible on a piece of scrap paper. I handed it to Ralph, who glanced at it and put it in his old, cracked leather wallet.

"I will let you know it I think of anything," Ralph said as he slipped his wallet back into his pocket.

I smiled at him and grabbed our empty glasses to bring back to the kitchen. When I reached the kitchen door, I looked back over my shoulder. The large man was still sitting on the couch, staring out the window at the bird feeders, his large hands folded in his lap.

As I squeezed some dish soap onto our glasses and started washing them in the sink, a voice came from the breakfast nook.

"You just can't leave well enough alone, can you?" my father said. He was sitting at the table looking at the Shady Lake Tribune, seemingly frozen in place from where I left him that morning. The only difference was that now he was eating a sandwich instead of scrambled eggs.

"Somebody has to help poor Ronald," I said. "Everyone is just acting like it is totally normal for Ronald to be a murder suspect and no one is doing anything to help him."

"That doesn't mean you should involve yourself in a murder investigation Tessa," he said. He stood up and walked over until he was directly in front of me. "Look, we are all feeling bad about Ronald. Most of the town believes he couldn't have done it. But what are we supposed to do?"

I didn't want to go round and round with him. I really didn't have the time to add "argue endlessly with my father" to my to do list. My dad gave me a big hug and kissed the top of my head. I squeezed him back.

"I'm still going to try to help," I said as I stepped out of his hug.

"I know," my dad said with a smile. "I knew you wouldn't stop, but I wouldn't be doing my job as a dad if I didn't tell you to stop."

We both laughed. Out of the entire family, I was the child that was the most like my dad. We were both stubborn as all get out, but also understood each other. Somehow, that meant that instead of fighting ourselves into a deadlock, we just let situations like this happen. We both knew how the other felt and that we weren't going to come to an agreement, so we agreed to disagree.

I turned and started to push open the door to the dining room. I need to get back to work. I wasn't sure where to start, but I had a million different things that needed to get done.

"Hey kid," my dad said.

I turned and looked at him.

"If you insist on staying involved, at least promise me that you will get Ronald out of jail," he said.

I smiled at him and nodded.

"I'll try my hardest," I said.

•Chapter 29•

I sat on the floor of the shed, surrounded by piles of pumpkins, lawn games, and wooden set ups that we were painting for all sorts of carnival games I'd dreamed up to keep the kids busy and raise more money at the Halloween Hayride. After I left my dad in the kitchen earlier today, I had decided that while I couldn't quit investigating, I needed to take a break from it. I especially needed a break since I had a mile-long list of things to do for the Halloween Hayride which was only two days away and I hadn't done a single one of them. That is when I had decided to call in reinforcements.

Mandy was painting a Halloween themed "go fish" booth where kids could throw their fishing lines over and someone behind would attach a piece of candy or a little Halloween tattoo. She was almost done painting a spooky underwater scene with skeleton fish. I giggled to myself when I spotted a streak of blue paint in her hair.

Clark and Max were actually working together to put the finishing touches on a wheel kids could spin to see what kind of candy they would win. I remembered this kind of stall always being very popular at school fun nights. Hopefully it would be popular for us also.

My parents were both organizing old Halloween accessories into a big plastic tote that we could use for a photo booth. With five kids and enough space that keeping stuff didn't mean a hoarding problem, they had tons of old Halloween costumes. Their job was to go through them all plus some stuff I had picked up at the second hand store and figure out what would make good props for a picture booth. They were finding some real gems like a plastic mask that had fake blood inside of it and a long hippie wig that badly needed brushing. I was thinking of throwing together a large display of pumpkins and maybe a sign that said "Happy Halloween" that people could pose in front of.

Tank and my other brother Teddy were packing the back of my station wagon with pumpkins that I was planning on driving out to the field the next day. My sisters would have been here if they could, but Trina was away at college and Tilly had to look after her kids while her husband was at work.

I looked around and realized how blessed I was. But in the next beat, I couldn't help but think of poor Ronald sitting in jail, probably wondering if I was keeping my word about the Halloween Hayride. I made a mental note to figure out if I was allowed to visit him or not. If I couldn't get him out, at least I could put his mind to rest about it.

"I think we're about done here," my dad said as he put the top on the plastic tote of dress up clothes. "Besides, it is getting late. If you need any more help, we can help you tomorrow."

"I will definitely need you to help me tomorrow," I said, standing up from the cross-legged position I had been sitting in for too long. I shook the pins and needles out of my feet. "We will need to get everything all set up out at the site."

"Why don't I meet you here around 5 tomorrow and we can drive our loads of stuff out to the field together," Clark suggested. His pick-up truck had already been commandeered as the other major transport vehicle for all of the Hayride stuff.

"That's a great plan," my dad said. "Anyone who can should meet here some time after work, around 5. We will transport as much as we can in one load and then most of us can stay out at the field and get stuff set up."

Mandy drifted out of the shed yawning while she waved at me and Tank and Teddy headed into the house along with my parents so that Tank could show Teddy the new guitar he had bought earlier in the week. I walked Clark and Max to their cars. Each one took their turn to give me a hug and a kiss on the cheek before hopping in their cars and driving off down the driveway.

I still had a few things I wanted to do, so I walked back into the shed to survey anything else that was left to do. I grabbed my to-do list and started checking off all of the things we had accomplished that night. We had actually managed to get most of the things done and I realized that all of the things left were things I either couldn't do until I was out at the field the next day or needed to be done when it was closer to Hayride time.

I started putting things away when a knock at the shed door made me jump.

"I'm sorry," Ralph said as he poked his head in the open door. "I didn't mean to scare you."

"Oh that's alright," I said. "It really

wasn't you that scared me. I was just deep in thought over this Halloween Hayride stuff and I didn't expect anyone else to be here."

Ralph walked inside. He started to walk slowly around, looking at all of the different things we had been working on. I wasn't quite sure why he was in the shed with me, but the thought crossed my mind that he was a very large man who had recently been the suspect in a murder and I was a somewhat petite female. I quickly pushed that thought out of my mind, telling myself that I had to stop listening to so many true crime podcasts.

"I'm not sure you realize how lucky you are to live in Shady Lake," Ralph finally said as he stopped in front of the fishing booth Mandy had been working on. He smiled to himself as he studied all of the details Mandy had included. There was even a little starfish skeleton that managed to be cute and make me laugh. "I grew up in a suburb of the Cities. It was a poor area and while many of the parents tried to do what they could to make out neighborhood welcoming, the reality was that they were busy trying to keep a roof over our heads and the city we were in didn't care about providing us with fun activities like this."

I had never really thought about it like that. When I moved to the big city, I had been an adult and fully enveloped in the brunch, fancy club, dinner at 9 sort of scene and never paid attention to any of the families that had been living around me.

But I understood the appeal of a small town to raise children. Shady Lake had been an amazing place to grow up. There were always programs for children during days off from school and the summer. The city was dotted all around with playgrounds and the streets were lined with sidewalks where families and children walked or rode their bikes.

"I would love to stay in a small town like this," he said. "Especially now that Susy and I have a baby on the way. But I don't think I'd be welcome in this one. Not after I was the first suspect in a murder."

"I don't think that's true," I said. "I would like to think we would welcome you with open arms. It might take some people a while to adjust, but over time I think it would be forgotten."

"It's a nice thought, but one I don't believe. Not after I've seen how no one is sticking up for Ronald."

I sighed and dropped my eyes to the floor. I knew he was right, even if I was trying to do something about it.

"But I know that you want to help," Ralph said. "That's why I'm here. I remembered something from the night of the murder."

My head snapped up to look at Ralph. He was shifting from foot to foot, looking down at the floor.

"What did you remember?" I asked. I couldn't stop my voice from shaking a little bit, but I tried to make it as level as possible. I wanted to seem somewhat professional.

"Well, it isn't much," he said. "I remembered that the car I saw in my rearview mirror was a lighter color and that when it turned into the field, the passenger's side door was smashed in like it had been in an accident sometime."

I repeated what he said in my head several times. It wasn't much to go on, but I decided to add it to my list of clues. Maybe I could start checking the body shops around here to see if any light colored cars came in with damage on the driver's side. But that would take a lot of time that I did not have. And I was on a timeline, if I wanted Ronald to be able to attend the Halloween Hayride.

"I hope that helps," Ralph said.

"I hope it does too," I said. "I'll definitely add it to my list of clues. Thank you for telling me."

Ralph nodded one curt nod of his head and walked out of the shed, leaving me surrounded by the Halloween spirit. I wandered over to a bench and sat down for a moment. In the next two days, I had to find the mysterious, light colored, damaged car, figure out who drives it, turn them in to the police, get Ronald released, all on top of setting up and running the Halloween Hayride. I may be in over my head a little bit.

•Chapter 30•

I opened my eyes the next morning not to my alarm, but to a text message on my phone. I looked at the clock and saw that it was only 6:15. Outside of my window it was pitch black still. The tree that was outside of my bedroom window had already lost a lot of leaves, so it stood eerie and looming. I hadn't seen it look so spooky for a while. Breakfast at the B&B wasn't served until closer to 8, so I usually didn't get up until shortly before that.

I blinked a few times and rubbed my eyes, trying to wake up a little bit. I had been up too late last night because I simply had too much on my mind to fall asleep until long past my bedtime. I had been running through the clues in my head and when that became too much, I ran through my to-do list of things that needed to get done for the Hayride.

After a few moments, I realized that I should probably check the message that had woken my up. If it was either Max or Clark, I was not going to be happy with them. They both knew I liked my sleep. I flipped open the phone to see.

I'm sorry to bother you so early, but I haven't been able to sleep. I have a huge favor to ask you. Please text me later.

I sleepily read the message over and over a few times, trying to figure out what it meant. I read it five times before I realized I had no idea who had sent me this message. I checked the sender and saw it came from Candy. I blinked a few times, wondering what in the world was going on.

I didn't mind helping Candy. I mean, she was going through a lot in her life and I had known her for a long time. She still seemed to be the same Candy as she had been in high school. I had felt bad for her then and I felt bad for her now. I just didn't understand why she had to ask for help so early in the morning. I typed out a short message.

Let me know what you need. I have to help serve breakfast at 8, but can help you for a short time after that.

It wasn't really great timing for Candy to need help. I hoped that whatever she needed would be short enough to fit in between all of the other things that I needed to get done today. I vowed that would say no if she wanted me to do anything too big. I needed to set my priorities straight. I shut my eyes just as my phone buzzed one more time. I groaned as I flipped it open to read the message.

Thank you. I'll text you later this morning.

I kind of wondered how Candy could take so much time away from work, especially considering her boss was currently in jail. I would think that would make her busier than ever before, but maybe everyone was cutting her slack seeing as how she was still grieving. I know that after Peter died, I was pretty much allowed to do whatever I wanted to. Well, I realize that in hindsight at least. When I was in the thick of it, I just tried to do everything I normally did how I normally did it and didn't realize until later how much everyone had been helping me pick up the slack.

After reading the last text from Candy, I realized there was no possible way I'd be able to go back to sleep now. So I rolled myself out of bed and got dressed in some casual, comfortable clothes because I knew I was going to be spending the entire day working on things. After I slipped on my most comfortable jeans, a shirt, and a nice sweatshirt I owned that didn't look too "sweatshirty," I stumbled my way downstairs to find a cup of coffee. This was the sort of morning where I really just wanted to set up a caffeine drip.

The morning managed to pass quickly. I helped serve breakfast to the guests and then I cleaned it up. I assigned a few of the things on the Hayride to-do list to some of the other members of the committee. I drank four cups of coffee, which was probably too many in too short of a time, but I blamed that on Candy and my early wakeup call.

Late morning, I hit a lull in my work where I realized I should probably see what Candy wanted me to help her with. I sent her a quick message. I worded it to make sure she understood that I was very busy and would be doing her a huge favor by agreeing to help her today.

Hey, I'm done with my work for now. I am really busy today, but I have a little bit of time depending on what you need. How can I help?

Candy must have been practically sitting on top of her phone because I immediately got a message back.

I really need to go out to the field. I need to see where Earl died and I need to see it before the Hayride gets all set up. Do you think you could give me a ride out there? My car is still out of commission.

I had been prepared to gently turn her request down because I was just so busy. But I did need to go out to the field. I could go drop off my load of pumpkins and have an empty car ready to transport more stuff this afternoon when we were all going to meet up. I hemmed and hawed back and forth before I sent a message back.

Okay. I have some things to bring out there anyways. Where can I pick you up?

I picked up my keys and wristlet wallet. I rarely bother with a purse unless I'm dressed up for a date or it's late at night and I need my flashlight along. I walked through the B&B to see if there was anyone around, but apparently everyone was out because the B&B was empty. I had already told my parents my plan for the day and they knew I was absolutely not available for anything today because of my long to-do list. I figured someone must be around to watch the desk and decided not to worry too much about it.

I'm at my house. Come whenever you can.

Once I slipped behind the wheel of my car, I happened to spot my father in an upstairs window. I gave him a wave. I could see him laugh a little as he waved back at me and I looked around to realize just how ridiculous I looked.

My station wagon was absolutely stuffed with pumpkins. I had very specifically told my brothers to not put any in the front seat because if it had been up to them, I would have been driving with a pumpkin on my lap and pumpkins as my co-pilot. Thank goodness they had listened to me, since Candy needed somewhere to sit.

I shrugged back at my father and turned on the car. I sat for a moment as my stuffed to the gills car threw me back in time to one of my favorite memories of Peter.

We only lived in two different apartments in the city because it was such a pain in the backside to move apartments. When we moved, we had actually borrowed the station wagon from my parents and stuffed it to the gills with out belongings. We didn't have much furniture, so that wasn't a problem. Our biggest problem was our giant, statement picture.

As a young, married couple, we had thought it was a great idea to buy a large, framed picture online. And when I say large, I mean it was as tall as me and just as wide. When it was delivered, we hung it as a statement piece above our couch and it looked amazing. Except then we had to move it. And unlike most things, you can't fold it or take it apart.

When we brought it out to the station wagon, we realized that it wasn't going to fit unless we really rigged it the right way. I was shorter, so we moved the bench seat as far forward as possible, rolled down the backseat windows so that the corners could stick out, and took the headrest off of the passenger seat. But I couldn't just carry it by myself once I got there, so Peter had laid down underneath the picture in the backseat and we had laughed all the way to the new apartment.

My beautiful, funny, loving Peter.

A tear rolled down my cheek and instead of just brushing it away as I wanted to, I acknowledged it and allowed myself to be sad, as my therapist had told me to do. I missed Peter every single day but over a year after his death, it doesn't hit me so hard every time. This wave of emotion had been a while coming, I think, pushed down by the emotions behind investigating a murder and organizing the Halloween Hayride.

I took a few deep breaths and just thought about Peter until the emotions passed. In an odd way, I realized that Candy and I actually had some things in common. Maybe I'd have to offer her some emotional help by way of a supportive shoulder and listening ear today.

But speaking of Candy, I needed to go pick her up and take her to the site of her boyfriend's murder.

•Chapter 31•

When I pulled up to the curb outside of Candy's small house, I sent a quick message to her to let her know I was outside. As I waited, I noticed there was a car in her driveway, tucked almost behind the house. It was a small, white car. The way it was parked in the driveway was awkward, almost as if she was trying to hide it in the backyard, but couldn't actually fit it behind the house.

I was pretty sure that Candy had previously said her car was in the shop. I had figured she was calling me because she didn't have a way to get out to the field. Maybe she just needed the emotional support and she knew I had been open to that recently. But why would she lie to me about her car?

The front door opened and Candy stepped outside, carrying a large purse. She waved with her keys in her hand and then turned to shut the door. As I watched the back of her as she locked the door, my mind flashed to what Ralph had said about the car he saw in the rearview mirror. It had been a light colored car and Candy drove a white car. I couldn't see the passenger door from here, so I didn't know if it was at all damaged. I didn't think it meant anything, but I took my phone out and sent a message to Mandy telling her what I was up to.

"Thank you so much for driving me," Candy said as she opened the door and slid inside. She gently set her purse down by her feet and buckled her seatbelt. "I just didn't want to go alone and I figured with the Halloween Hayride starting tomorrow, that you would need to go out there anyways. Judging from your car, you certainly do need to take a trip out there."

I giggled once again at the ridiculous thought of me rolling around town in my own, metal pumpkin patch. Door to door pumpkin selling might be an easy way to make money.

"Yeah, sorry about all the pumpkins," I said. "Just be glad you have somewhere to sit. If it were up to my brothers, you would have had to ride on the roof."

I laughed again and Candy laughed a polite sort of laugh, but when I looked at her, the happiness didn't reach her eyes. She was having to force a laugh. I understood. Sometimes when you are grieving, it is hard to realize that the rest of the world is still turning, moving on while you are stuck grasping on to your loved one through memories.

I reached over and grabbed Candy's hand. She was shaking a little bit, but she let me give her hand a squeeze. I figured this might be a good time to try and connect emotionally with her.

"Candy, I know what you are feeling right now," I said. "I've been there. I still think about Peter everyday. But let me just tell you that you will feel better. Every day will get a little easier than the one before and one day you will remember how to breath."

Candy shut her eyes and took a deep breath in. She kept grasping my hand and taking shaky breaths in and out. She kept squeezing her eyelids shut tight to push back tears that were forming. After a few moments, she looked up at me. She had an odd expression on her face that I couldn't quite read.

"Thank you Tessie," she said. "I just really needed to see where Earl spent his last moments and I thought you'd be the perfect person to go with me."

"Of course Candy, I'm here to help. I do have one question though. I thought you said you were getting your car fixed. Isn't that your car right there in your driveway?"

Candy furrowed her eyebrows together for a moment before exaggeratedly nodding her head a few times.

"Oh, the car, yeah," she said with a nervous laugh. "I did get it back. I suppose I could have driven myself, but I just really needed someone to come with me."

I could somewhat understand that. But I was pretty uneasy with how Candy was acting. She didn't seem distant so much as she felt like she was hiding something. I got the idea that she and Earl weren't quite as happy together as she may have tried to make them seem. After all, they did have the argument on the morning of his murder.

"Well, shouldn't we get going?" Candy said with a laugh. Her eyes darted back and forth. "I know you are really busy today. Let's go deliver these pumpkins."

Candy gave a nervous laugh that was a bit disarming to hear. I put the car in drive and started to slowly pull back into the street. I rolled slowly past Candy's house and tried to sneakily look at Candy's car as we went by. I was wondering if she was trying to hide something about her car. It looked like she had backed it into her driveway and then backed as far behind her house as she possibly could. I just needed to see the passenger side of it and compare to the car Ralph had seen at the field.

I couldn't quite see the side of her car so I decided to pull into Candy's driveway and pretend I wanted to turn around and go the other way. I felt kind of dumb going to such lengths to just look at the side of someone's car, but I knew if I didn't, I wouldn't be able to think of anything else all day. It would bother me all day that I hadn't seen the side of her car.

The car pulled forward up the driveway and I let it pull forward much further than I normally would so that the front of my car was almost hitting the front of Candy's car. I leaned forward a little bit and tried to look like I was stretching a little bit.

"Oh hold on," I muttered. I put the car in park and turned to Candy. "I need to check my headlights real quick. I thought I saw one of them go out on the way over here."

It was just barely cloudy enough to maybe need headlights, but it was the best thing I could come up with on the fly. I surreptitiously switched my headlights on before hopping out of the car. I leaned back down before I closed the door.

"It'll just take me a second," I said. "I'm going to be doing a lot of nighttime driving out in the country during the Halloween Hayride, so if I have a headlight out, I want to change it as soon as possible."

Candy scowled at me from the passenger seat, but nodded at me. I think she knew I was lying, but she didn't know how to call me on it. I guess it was similar to me not knowing how to call her out for lying about her car. We were kind of in a stalemate.

I walked to the front of my car and glanced at both headlights. I held up a finger to indicate "just a minute" to Candy in the car and I squatted down like I was inspecting something closely. I hoped Candy didn't really understand cars otherwise she would wonder what in the world I was doing.

Finally I had a clear shot to look at the passenger side of her car. One glance at the side of the car and I could see a giant dent caving in the entire side of the passenger door. This was the car Ralph had seen turning into the field after he left Earl just before he was murdered. Candy had been out at the field at the time that Earl was murdered.

•Chapter 32•

I got back into the car and I must have paused a beat too long before I shifted the car into reverse because Candy turned and looked at me. Her eyes were wide and her expression was blank. She smiled a large, disarming smile, but there was a coldness behind it that made mt consider whether I wanted to actually drive her out into the middle of nowhere.

I tried to always listen to my gut feeling, but right now my gut feeling was a bit conflicted. Candy was definitely acting strange, but she could just be figuring out her own emotions while still very fresh in the grieving process. Maybe she was out at the field for a totally innocent reason and she left before Earl was murdered. I would have to ask her.

For now, I decided I should drive her to the field. She was grieving and needed some help. I had to be at the field anyway to drop off these stupid pumpkins.

As I drove, I tried to keep my nervousness down by fiddling with the radio knobs, the heat vents, anything while I tried to figure out what I should do. I turned up the country and western that was on and tried to sing along even though part of the way through I realized it wasn't even a song I really knew. I had turned the heat way up and then had to turn it down when I started sweating. But Candy must have noticed.

"What's wrong Tessie," Candy said. "I thought you were really busy. We really need to be going."

My heart leapt into my throat, but I managed to swallow it down while I rolled down her driveway and down the street.

"I'm alright," I said. "I was just thinking of a question I had for you and I was wondering if it was appropriate to ask it."

Candy tilted her head and gave me an odd look. She looked befuddled, but I still got a sense that she was hiding something from me.

"You can ask me anything Tessie," she said. "I feel like we are fabulous friends."

I swallowed down the lump in my throat and decided to just get right to it without beating around the bush.

"I was just wondering if you were out at the field at all the night that Earl was murdered?"

My question was met with total silence

that was really telling. I had hoped she would just think I was silly asking her that question and would play it off, but instead she wasn't saying anything. I sneaked a glance at Candy, who had a large smile frozen on her face. She was staring through me, but her right hand kept moving jerkily back and forth to touch and stroke her purse at her feet.

"You're the first person I have told, but yes I was," she said.

I pulled into the field and parked the car in front of the main shed that housed the tractor. I shut the car off and turned to look at Candy. She was still staring at me, but her eyes had changed. Her eyes were hard now, boring into me. I was thoroughly worried now.

"When were you here?" I asked, even though I already thought I knew the answer.

"That's not important," Candy said. "What is important is that we are here now and you can show me where you found Earl's body. I want to see it."

Candy opened her door and stepped out, throwing her purse strap over her head. As she marched around the car to my side, I quickly grabbed my phone and punched a few buttons. Candy threw my car door open and grabbed my sleeve. I was surprised at how strong her grip was.

"Get out of the car," she said with a snarl.

I stepped my foot out onto the gravel drive and tried to hide my phone in my hand as I stood up, but Candy spotted it. She grabbed it out of my hand. For a moment, she looked almost confused by the fact that I had a flip phone.

"You won't be needing this," she said as she turned it over and over in her hand. "We're all friends here."

Her eyes were wide and wild, looking every which way. I took a closer look at Candy and realized that she was looking a bit rougher than normal. Her normally perfectly styled, platinum hair was frizzier than normal and sticking up all over. While her style was normally a bit out of place, she was usually somewhat put together. Today her shirt had sweat stains under her arms and it was a bit stretched out in the neckline. Her jeans had tears in them and not fashionable tears, but the kind that come from doing manual labor.

I stood up as she slipped my phone into her pocket. I didn't ever think I would be scared of Candy. But this was not the

Candy that I had known.

"Let's go," Candy said.

She grabbed my arm and started marching towards the shed that had the tractor in it, dragging me behind her. She was clutching her purse in her other hand. Her hair was sticking up in all directions and every time she looked at me, her eyes were darting all over the place.

"Candy, are you okay?" I asked. " Listen, I know what it is like to lose your partner. I know that you said you were planning on marrying Earl. I lost my husband Peter. I can help you. I know what you are feeling right now."

Candy stopped in her tracks so abruptly that I ran into the back of her. She turned slowly and looked at me.

"You don't know what I'm feeling," she said. "No one really knows what I'm feeling."

She started walking again and stopped in front of the shed.

"Open up the shed and let's get on the tractor," she said.

I got out the keys and opened the lock before throwing the doors open. The orange tractor was sitting exactly where it should be. I walked in and climbed up onto the tractor. Candy climbed up behind me and stood on a little platform behind the driver's seat. She gripped my shoulders with her unnaturally strong grip. There was on way I was going to get off of this tractor until Candy let me get off of it.

"Let's go," she said. "Drive me out to where Earl died."

"Don't you know how to drive the tractor?" I asked.

"Don't you think I would already be driving this thing if I did?" she sneered.

I wasn't in a position to argue, so I started the tractor up and put it into drive. It rolled out of the shed and I drove it as close as I could remember to where it had been the night we found Earl.

"This is it," she said. "This is where he died, right?"

I looked around, but without the tractor already sitting there or the police tape still up for reference, I had no idea where Earl's body had been that dark night. I sort of shrugged my shoulders and hoped my answer didn't disappoint Candy.

"This is the spot," Candy said quietly when I didn't answer. Her face was blank. The mania had slipped off of her face without leaving another expression behind.

"This is where he died," she said in a whisper. She let go of my shoulders and stared at the ground.

I started to try and climb off of the tractor to put some distance between us, but Candy abruptly grabbed my shoulders and sat me back down.

"Stop right there," she said. "I wouldn't move anywhere if you know what's good for you."

"I was just going to go unload some of the pumpkins and give you some privacy," I said. For once, my quick mouth came up with something good instead of just getting me into trouble.

"I don't need privacy," Candy said. "I just need you to stay here. In fact, I need you to stay here forever."

I looked at her quizzically. Was she having a breakdown? I didn't know what she wanted and it was unnerving me.

"Candy, why don't we go get a coffee and you can take a break," I said. "It sounds like you might need a little bit of time to get yourself back together. I can help you set up a break from work."

I took a chance and quickly hopped down off of the tractor to start walking back to the car. Candy bent down and grabbed my shoulder to yank me back towards her with almost inhuman strength. Her long fingernails dug into my skin, even through the layers I was wearing.

"You're going the wrong way," Candy said.

I turned to look at her. She opened up her purse and pulled out a small pistol that had been tucked inside.

"It's all gone too far now," she said. "I can't have you running to your boyfriend to tell him everything. For a while, I thought it would all be okay because you thought the watch was Ronald's, but I know you've put everything together now. I can't have you telling everyone else. You've been the only one smart enough to put it all together. Now I need you to walk the opposite way and stand in front of the tractor."

I gasped involuntarily. The watch I had found was Candy's, not Ronald's. Candy was right about one thing. All of the clues were falling into place now.

●Chapter 33●

Her hand let go of my shoulder, but she kept the pistol pointed at me. Her empty hand was shaking, but she somehow managed to keep the pistol leveled at me. I swallowed hard and followed her directions.

"Candy, what is going on?"

"I can't take any chances," she said. "I didn't do anything wrong. I can't have you ruining everything I did to protect myself. Everything was just a big accident. No one can know what happened."

"Maybe I can help you," I said. I knew I needed to keep her talking. I needed to stall as much as possible. "Tell me what happened and I can help you figure out a plan. I won't tell anyone about this."

Candy shook her head violently back and forth. More of her hair spilled out of her ponytail around her shoulders. A few tears were leaking out of her eyes and falling down her face to where her teeth were clenched together.

"If you're going to kill me, you might as well tell me," I said. "A confession always feels good and it'll feel even better to give it to someone who will be dead in a few minutes."

She stared unblinking at me for a few moments while I tried hard to look her straight in the eye. I wanted her to see me and think about what she was threatening to do.

"Okay, I'll tell you," Candy said. "But only because I've known you so long that I think you deserve an explanation."

I nodded. I was working hard on breathing through my nose and keeping a neutral expression. Candy was obviously volatile and I didn't feel like poking the bear any more than I already had.

"The morning before Earl died, we had an argument," Candy said. "I had seen him having coffee with another woman. When I asked him about it, he wouldn't tell me much about it. He just brushed it off like it was nothing. But if it was nothing, why wouldn't he just explain to me what was going on? I just wanted him to reassure me that I was his girl, but instead he got all defensive. We were supposed to get married."

Candy started pacing a little bit. She was waving the gun around as she gestured wildly, but always kept it pointed in my direction. Her face was starting to get red now as she immersed herself in the memory of the fight.

"Earl had mentioned that he and Ralph were coming out here to cause some mischief that night, so when I just couldn't stop thinking about our fight, I decided to come out here and confront him. I saw that woman driving around out here when I was pulling up and I figured she had been out here with him. I was so mad that he was still lying to me."

I realized suddenly that the other woman Candy had seen with Earl was Susy, his cousin. She had absolutely no idea that Earl's problem wasn't an affair, but money issues. Of course Earl would keep her in the dark about it. He couldn't let her know that he wasn't as successful as he let others think he was. He was no dummy. He would have figured out that the biggest reason Candy was with him was for his money.

"So I drove in here and he was all by himself," Candy said. "I jumped out of my car and found him out by the tractor. He was trying to get it stuck in the mud or something, but he had no idea how to actually drive a tractor. I offered to do it. I didn't really know how to do it, but I couldn't resist showing him up a little. I mean, I'm from a little country town. I should have been able to figure it out. Then when I was up there, I told him he should dig down by the front tire to get it stuck down in the mud."

I shifted my weight from one foot to the other. Candy immediately leveled the gun at me and scowled before she continued her story.

"Earl was an idiot," she said. "I loved him, but he was an idiot. He thought I was some ditzy blond who would do whatever he said. So when he got close to the wheel, I rolled it forward and I was lucky that it was just enough to trap his toes underneath."

Candy started to cry a little more. I put my hand in my pocket and she waved the gun at me until I pulled a tissue out and handed it to her. Her muttered 'thank you' let me know she wasn't too far gone yet.

"Once I had him trapped, I told him I'd seen the other woman. I'd seen her at the coffee shop and I'd seen her in her car as I was on my way out here. I told him that I wouldn't stand for it. There was no way I'd let a man step out on me. He started muttering on about it not being what I thought it was and he could explain it all to me."

Her voice started to shake and she took a minute to compose herself. When she spoke again, her voice was so quiet I could hardly hear her.

"I wasn't sure I believed him, but then he said he wanted to spend the rest of his life with me. And I realized that I should give him another chance. So I hopped out of the seat to give him a kiss, but I forgot to put the tractor into park. As I turned to jump down off of the tractor, it lurched forward and ran over Earl."

By now, Candy was sobbing and I even found a few tears falling down my face. I almost wanted to reach out and comfort her, until I remember the gun she still had pointed at me.

"I didn't mean for it to happen," she said. "I really didn't. I loved Earl."

I believed her. I really did believe that she loved Earl. But I had to tell her what I knew about him. I still needed more time.

"Candy, I know the woman that you saw with Earl," I said. If she was going to kill me, I at least wanted her to know the truth. "That woman was Earl's cousin, Susy. She was here in Shady Lake to try and force Earl to sell her the business and field."

All of the color drained from Candy's face until her previously red face was left ghostlike. She started jerkily shaking her head back and forth.

"No, that can't be right," she said as she lowered the gun to her side. "Earl would have just told me that. Why would he keep that from me? You must be lying."

"I'm not lying to you, Candy. Susy is staying at the bed and breakfast right now. I've talked to her and she told me all about meeting Earl to try and talk him into selling to her. She also admitted she tried to follow Earl out here that night, but she had to stop and she lost track of him."

Candy staggered backward a step and doubled over with her hands on her knees. My news had socked her right I the gut. For a moment, I thought she was going to be sick, but instead she took a few deep breaths before standing back up straight. Candy slowly brought her gun back up to point it straight at me again.

"That just makes this so much harder," Candy said. "Killing Earl was an accident, but now I have to kill you too. And it turns out I have to do all of this over a mistake. What a waste this all was. I'm sorry Tessie. I really do like you."

That's when I heard the sirens in the distance. I heard them just a split second before Candy did. It was the one time in my life that I was glad to hear a police car screaming towards me.

"Why are you smiling?" she snarled at me. "I have to kill you."

I looked over my shoulder and saw multiple squad cars barreling towards us down the gravel driveway, lights flashing and sirens blaring. One look at Candy and I could see that she was momentarily distracted, so I started running as fast as I could towards the sheds and I didn't stop until the lead squad car drove right up on my right side. The passenger door flew open and Mandy appeared in the open space.

"Jump in," she yelled.

I dove in and curled up in her lap as two more squad cars pulled up on either side of us. Max leaned over from the driver's seat and kissed my forehead.

"My knight in shining armor," I smiled up at him.

"I'm just glad you're safe," he said. "Now I have to go bring her in."

Max jumped out of the car and Mandy squeezed me tight as we watched. As the officers ran towards Candy, she dropped the gun and put her hands in the air. She was sobbing and her hair was sticking in all directions. The officers approached with their guns drawn until they were able to grab her.

Mandy turned and looked at me. She kept trying to form a question, but didn't quite know what to say.

"What happened?" she finally said.

"I'll tell you everything, but I need three things first," I said. "I need those pumpkins unloaded out of my car and then I need a giant cup of coffee and a donut."

•Chapter 34•

I drove my now empty station wagon to the Donut Hut with Mandy. We didn't even have to talk. We just listened to Don drone along on the radio as I drove. The soothing baritone helped me come back down to earth once the adrenaline stopped pumping. When I walked in the front door of the cafe, the shop was filled with my parents and siblings. Even my sister Trina who is away at college was there over video chat. The shop was warm and filled with laughter and good cheer.

When I walked in, I was rushed by my family. Everyone took a turn to give me a hug before they escorted me to a a a seat at a large table they'd made by pushing together the small tables. Everyone was clamoring for me to tell the story. As I sat down, Mandy pushed a Halloween donut and a mug of coffee in front of me.

"Hold on everyone, I will tell you all what happened," I said. "But first, I really need this."

I lifted my mug to my lips and took a long drink of coffee. The warmth spread down my throat and all through my body as my family laughed. They all knew I loved coffee, but after staring down the barrel of a gun, I really needed a strong cup of coffee. The warmth helped as I realized my fingers were half frozen from being out in the field for so long.

As I ate, Mandy brought out donuts and coffee for everyone. I made a mental note to pay her for all of this later on. Once I felt full of caffeine and sugar, I told them the entire story of finding out Candy was the murderer, from picking her up at her house and discovering the dent on her car to driving the tractor for her to her admitting the truth right before the police showed up. When I got to the end of my story, my mother chuckled a little as she raised her hand slightly into the air.

"I have a question," she said as the group tittered. "How did the police and Mandy know you were in danger?"

"I think Mandy should answer that while I have another donut," I said.

I grabbed another donut and took a big bite. Tomorrow I'd go back to try to limit the amount of donuts I eat daily. But today I faced down death and I was going to eat as many donuts as I wanted to. Mandy came over with a carafe of coffee and filled my cup.

"Tessa sent me a text message that just said *In danger. Get police. Field,*" Mandy said. "I've known Tessa long enough to know that she wasn't joking around. Thankfully, Max was actually here in the shop having a donut, so I was able to show him the message and get him out there just in the nick of time."

"Okay, just one more question," a voice in the back said. I had been so preoccupied up until this point that I hadn't noticed the bush of red hair in the back of the crowd. As Chelsea spoke, the crowd parted to let her through. Judging by her pen and notepad, she had been writing down everything I had said.

"Chelsea, this isn't a press conference," I said as I rolled my eyes. "But I suppose you can write about this."

"When in the world did you manage to send a message to Mandy?" she asked. The way Chelsea was asking was making it sound like she thought I was lying. I hoped she didn't sound like this at any of her other interviews. "After you picked up Candy, you were driving and then you said that she almost immediately took your phone. So when were you able to send that message?"

I thought back to earlier that afternoon. I had started to have the gut feeling that something was wrong as soon as I pulled up to pick up Candy. Even before I saw the dented car or even talked to Candy, the pit of my stomach had an odd feeling that I just couldn't shake. So as I was bent down pretending I was looking at the headlights, I quickly made a draft text message to Mandy, but didn't send it until we got to the field. I had just enough time as Candy walked around the car to hit send and get the message to Mandy.

"I guess we all know what we'll see on the front page of the paper tomorrow," my brother Teddy joked. Everyone laughed as Chelsea blushed.

"Okay everyone, press conference over," I said before taking another big bite of donut.

Everyone laughed and started milling around again. I stood up and walked over to Chelsea as I chewed up the bite I had just taken. She was hurriedly packing up her bag, but I managed to catch her by the elbow.

"Hey, you're only going to hear me say this once," I said. "But you do a great job reporting at the paper. I'm glad you are the one who will be writing this story."

Chelsea smiled at me. Her shoulders relaxed and she stopped shoving things into her backpack.

"Thanks Tess," she said. "And you'll only hear me say this once. You did a great job solving this murder and I'm glad you gave me something exciting to write about for once."

I smiled at her one more time before I felt a large arm wrap itself around my waist. I turned around to find myself face to face with Max.

"Hello Officer Marcus," I said. "I bet it isn't often that you come to the aid of a damsel in distress."

Max laughed and pulled me close to him.

"Stop teasing," he said quietly. "You aren't a damsel in distress. You just forgot to bring a gun to the fight apparently."

He leaned down and gave me a quick peck on the lips. Normally a peck on the lips would seem so ordinary and common place, but today it was the most romantic gesture in the world, especially considering that Max was still technically on duty.

"Now I have to report back to duty," Max said as he walked away. "Something about an extraordinary woman citizen solving a murder this morning I have to go deal with."

Max pushed the front door open and glanced back over his shoulder, throwing me a beaming smile. I smiled back before noticing the clock above the door. My heart leapt into my throat as I realized there were only a few hours left until the Halloween Hayride started.

I found the nearest chair and stood up on top of it. As I cleared my throat, everyone looked up at me.

"Attention everyone," I said with my hands cupped around my mouth. "As it appears none of you have anything better to do this afternoon, I am signing you all up for the Halloween Hayride set-up crew which is going to be meeting as soon as we all drive out to the field. So, if you have a small car, please meet me at the field. If you have a large vehicle, please go to my house to load up with stuff. Thank you."

Once again, the crowd laughed, but I was pleased to hear them making plans about who was riding in which car as they made their way out the door.

"I've got to hand it to you. You have done a good job taking over the Halloween Hayride."

I turned around to see Ronald standing

with his hands in his pockets. Melinda was scowling next to him. Together, they looked like they should be in a children's book about opposites. I ran over and gave him a big squeeze.

"I'm so glad to see you," I said happily. "But I'm going to come right out and ask you because I just have to know: if the watch I found was Candy's, where in the world is your watch?"

Ronald looked around nervously. He seemed to be making sure that Melinda was out of earshot before he leaned forward and whispered to me.

"That night I was supposed to go to the gym and walk on the track for some exercise," Ronald said. "Instead, Earl made me so mad that I drove to the truck stop and bought a giant jelly donut. When I took the first bite, jelly squirted out all over my watch and I couldn't clean it off. I didn't want Mellie to know about the donut, so I hid it from her. I couldn't say what happened to it because otherwise Mellie would know. I didn't want to disappoint her because I'm trying so hard."

"I'm just glad they let you out in time for the Hayride," I said. I knew the secret of the watch had something to do with Melinda. I was just glad to hear it had to do with a jelly donut, no matter how ridiculous that may be.

"Me too, but it appears they didn't have to," Ronald said, his eyes twinkling. "You've done a fine job of making sure it still goes on as planned. And you've shown me that maybe I can loosen my grip on some of the town's traditions so others have a chance to step up and take over. But mostly, I just wanted to say thank you. Now, if you'll excuse me, I will meet you at the field."

I smiled at him as he turned to walk away. After he was out of hearing range, Melinda grabbed my sleeve with her claw like hand. I was about to protest when she spoke.

"Thank you," she said. "I know everyone thinks I'm never happy, but the one thing that always makes me happy is Ronald. I'm forever indebted to you for getting him out of jail."

Before I could say anything, Melinda was gone. She trailed behind in Ronald's wake as they exited the Donut Hut. I knew she would be scowling out at the Halloween Hayride field soon.

And now I knew why she was always with

Ronald, even if she did have a sour look on her face the entire time.

•Chapter 35•

The first couple of loads of hayride people had already been driven through the course, so I was finally able to relax a little bit. It could take a while for everything and everyone to get into a good groove, but so far they'd had all happy customers.

After my triumphant retelling at the Donut Hut, I had over twenty people help me transport things out to the field and get them set up for the Halloween Hayride. We finished set up even earlier than I had previously planned because of all of the extra help.

Now Max and I were sitting in two of the chairs set out by the food stand and watching everyone go by. We had gotten a pretty good ribbing when we had ordered our hot dogs in our ketchup and mustard costumes, but we laughed along at the absurdity of it all. Now we were comfortable in our chairs next to a fire barrel enjoying the last of our hot dogs as we watched everyone walk by. Every few minutes, someone would stop to congratulate me and Max on catching Earl's killer. After the fifth time, Max rolled his eyes at me after the well wishers left.

"You'd think we were some ace police duo," he said. "But this is the first and last murder investigation you'll solve."

For now, I happily munched down the last bites of my hot dog and watched the kids in costumes that were running by. By this point in my life, I thought I'd probably have a few kids of my own. And weirdly enough at one point, I figured I'd have them with the guy sitting next to me. Life was funny that way.

I looked at Max in his ridiculous head to toe red outfit and wondered if he was thinking the same thing. More than likely, he was thinking about whether he should eat another hot dog. He had always had a bottomless pit of a stomach.

"Well, I see you stuck with that ridiculous condiment theme you initially suggested to me," Clark said as he strolled up. He was dressed as a cowboy. He had certainly picked a more handsome costume than I had made Max dress up in. "Good thing you found someone to agree to it."

Clark started laughing until Max elbowed him in the side. He doubled over a bit and I laughed along with them until I noticed Chelsea walking up behind Clark. She was dressed in a cowgirls outfit with cowboy boots and a big cowboy hat over two red braids. She was holding a steaming cup of hot cider in each hand.

"Oh hi there," she said coyly. "I was just looking for my cowboy."

She winked at Clark, who chuckled nervously as he grabbed his cup of cider from her. So this is what Chelsea had meant when she was being so mysterious about Clark. I couldn't be mad at Clark, but I had to wonder if he picked her simply because we don't get along.

"Ah, I see you found someone to be your cowgirl after I turned you down," I said before I could stop myself. No matter how nice I had been to Chelsea earlier, I wasn't going to let her think she got the last word.

Chelsea scowled at me as Clark kicked at a few rocks. Max couldn't help but grin at everyone. He was the winner in their unofficial competition this time.

"We need to go get in line for the Hayride," Chelsea said as she grabbed Clark's arm. "Come on, let's go."

Chelsea marched away, dragging Clark by the sleeve. Clark looked back apologetically and waved goodbye. No matter what, neither he nor Max had won.

There was no winning because it wasn't a competition. It was all just fun and games.

Max reached over and grabbed my hand. For a while, we just sat holding hands. The warmth from the fire barrel was just enough to stop me from shivering. I was just thinking of how good that hot cup of cider had looked when I noticed Susy and Ralph holding hands next to a large stack of pumpkins.

"Hold on Max. I'll be right back."

I stood up and walked over to where they were whispering back and forth to each other. As I walked, I had to wave off several more well-wishers, but I was determined to talk to Susy and Ralph before I lost them in the crowd. When they saw me, both of them beamed at me.

"Hi Tessa, we were just saying we hoped we saw you here," Susy said. Ralph nodded along. He was looking happier than ever. "We both wanted to thank you for helping to clear Ralph's name. This situation was just what we needed to figure out our relationship once and for all."

"I'm so glad to hear that," I said. I couldn't help but be a little nosy. "What did you have to figure out?"

"Well, we've decided we are going to get

married," Ralph said. "Nothing fancy or anything. And we want to try to stick around down here. Susy has the car lot now and we can run that together while we take care of the kids."

I couldn't help but smile as Ralph put his hand on Susy's stomach. Nothing physically gave away the pregnancy yet, but Susy was positively glowing. They looked so perfect together that I just knew I should capture the moment.

"Congratulations!" I said. "Hand me one of your phones, you both need a picture of this happy moment."

Ralph took out his smart phone, brought up the camera app and handed it to me. He stepped back next to Susy. They turned to face each other and Ralph put his oversized hand gently on her stomach. Susy put her hand on his waist. They weren't actually ready, but I snapped a few pictures because you could practically see the love floating back and forth between them. I also snapped one once they were in position and smiling at me.

"We will have to celebrate sometime," I said as I handed Ralph his phone back. "For now, I should be getting in line to ride the hayride. I suppose the head of the Hayride

committee should actually ride the
hayride."

I turned to look for Max, but the chair he
had been sitting in was empty. Before I
could even wonder where he was, I spotted
my red clad man coming towards me with
two steaming cups of our own hot cider.
Max was so good at predicting what small
things would make me happy. He handed
me the hot cup and I blew on it a few times
before taking a satisfying drink of the hot,
cinnamon tasting beverage.

"That hits the spot," I said, trying not to
gulp it all down and burn my mouth. "How
did you get these so fast? The line at the
food stand is so long."

"They looked so good when Chelsea
brought her cups over that I knew we
needed some too," Max said. "All I had to
do was flash the badge a few times to get to
the front."

I narrowed my eyes at Max before he
backtracked. He burst into giggles.

"Kidding, kidding. But I may have
mentioned that one of the cups was for the
head of the Halloween Hayride committee."

I had to laugh as we headed towards the
line for the hayride, but when we got there I
was quickly ushered to the front of the line.

I used my best Minnesotan excuses, but I knew nothing would stand up against the fact that I had caught a murderer today and still managed to spearhead the Hayride. So I accepted my fast track up to the front.

When the hayride came back around to pick up the next group, I was ushered to the prized spot at the front of the wagon. Max and I settled in and tucked one of the provided plaid blankets over out legs to keep out the cold as we rode through the spooky scenes.

As the wagon drove through the course, it drove through several scenes. I snuggled up next to Max as we drove through a medieval torture chamber complete with a stretching rack and then the dungeon of a mad scientist who was bringing to life some sort of creepy monster. Everyone on the hayride was laughing and chatting back and forth, alternatively jumping from people popping out from behind sets and trees and giggling about the silly parts of the hayride.

As I looked around at everything, I had to admit that Ralph had been right. I was lucky to grow up in Shady Lake and I was lucky to be living here now. Small town Minnesota might not be everyone's cup of tea, but right now it was my hot cup of cider.

•About the Author•

Linnea West lives in Minnesota with her husband and two children. She taught herself to read at the age of four and published her first poem in a local newspaper at the age of seven. After a turn as a writer for her high school newspaper, she went to school for English Education and Elementary Education. She didn't start writing fiction until she was a full time working mother. Besides reading and writing, she spends her time chasing after her children, watching movies with her husband, and doing puzzle books. Learn more about her and her upcoming books by visiting her website and signing up for her newsletter at linneawestbooks.com.

Note From the Author: Reviews are gold to authors! If you've enjoyed this book, would you consider rating it and reviewing it on Amazon? Thank you!

●Other Books in the Series●

Small Town Minnesota Cozy Mystery Series

Book One-Halloween Hayride Murder
Book Two-Christmas Shop Murder
Book Three-Winter Festival Murder

Made in the USA
Middletown, DE
01 February 2019